Outside

PROVIDENCE

ALSO BY PETER FARRELLY

The Comedy Writer

Outside
PROVIDENCE

Peter Farrelly

D O U B L E D A Y
New York   London   Toronto   Sydney   Auckland

A Main Street Book

PUBLISHED BY DOUBLEDAY
a division of Bantam Doubleday Dell Publishing Group, Inc.
1540 Broadway, New York, New York 10036

MAIN STREET BOOKS, DOUBLEDAY, and the portrayal of a building with a tree are
trademarks of Doubleday, a division of Bantam Doubleday Dell Publishing Group, Inc.

BOOK DESIGN BY LYNNE AMFT

Library of Congress Cataloging-in-Publication Data
Farrelly, Peter.
Outside Providence / Peter Farrelly.—1st Main Street Books ed.
p.   cm.
"A Main Street Book"—T.p. verso.
I. Title.
PS3556.A7725O98   1998
813'.54—dc21   98-15443
CIP

ISBN 0-385-49058-5

First Main Street Books Edition: November 1998

1   3   5   7   9   10   8   6   4   2

For my parents and for Cordo Wilford

Outside PROVIDENCE

PART *One*

Dildo,

that's what my old man called me. Dildo Dunphy. I remember when he dubbed me. It was a muggy day in the summer of my ninth year and I'd run inside his radiator shop to borrow fifteen cents for a frozen lemonade. The old man blotted his forehead with the back of his hand and leaned against the counter, the tiny blood vessels on his nose gorged red with rancor. He scowled over a bogus Jimmy Fund bucket and said, "Until you earn it, *Dildo,* just stay the hell out of here!"

My Christian name is Timothy Brian Dunphy and I was born and raised in Pawtucket, Rhode Island, a rotting city bleeding off an anemic river just north of Providence. The old man loved Pawtucket. Claimed it had flavor. I couldn't argue with that; the city smelled like a sour-cream-and-onion-flavored potato chip, on account of the Choo-Sum junk food factory a mile upstream. Factory City, U.S.A., that's what Pawtucket was called in her prime.

My old man and brother and I lived on the first floor of a seventy-year-old triple-decker perched above the tire-and-barrel-strewn banks of the Blackstone River. The apartments above us had been condemned and were occupied by bats. Life as we know it had left the Blackstone years earlier, although occasionally there were rumors that someone had spotted a three-headed frog or a giant Siamese carp swimming near one of the factories. I never swam in the Blackstone.

My mother hadn't lived with us since November 22, 1963. That's when she blew her brains all over our garage. Don't let the date weigh you down; it's not the reason, just fueled her mood. On our front door was a handgun-shaped sticker that read: FORGET THE DOG—BEWARE OF THE OWNER.

The neighborhood consisted of Nielsen families, I suppose. Another lady on my street committed side-sui; my next-door neighbor was doing time for being an accessory to a murder; about one-third of the parents were divorced; another third were screwing around; there were a couple of wife beaters; a few child abusers; a possible husband beater; a good crew of alkies; and the nut at the top of the street was on probation for bumblasting a troop of Boy Scouts.

The intersection in front of our house was the most hazardous in the state. It was a five-wayer regulated by a huge, pentagonal traffic light that winked an enticing yellow in each direction. At rush hour it became a five-army battle to see which battalion of cars would blast through first. One year there were more than fifty fender-benders. To the old man's chagrin, though, there'd never been a real grisly wreck—a lot of close calls but no corpses. We all knew it was coming. Sort of like living on a fault line; we were always waiting for the Big One.

I'm six feet tall with curly, dark red hair. I don't have freckles. When I was younger, the old man used to proudly tell me that redheaded guys are supposed to have mean streaks. He was confident that I would sprout into a short-tempered wild man. Well, I didn't have it. I looked for it, I *prayed,* I dug deep into my soul, but it wasn't there. I used to stand in front of the bathroom mirror before bedtime and grimace and snarl and flex my nostrils and wrinkle my lips, but I couldn't convince myself that I was to be feared. When someone would pick a fight with me, I'd get all set—stand sideways and crouch as if protecting a manly set of balls—and I'd be staring at the kid I was supposed to be wailing on; but all I could see was my own puffy face and my little grapes, and before I could shake the image the kid would knuckle me. After years of getting beaten up for not being mean enough, my face finally developed the thick mean look that the old man promised. Girls, for the most part, didn't notice me, but the few I did hook up with credited my good fortune to the "cute chip" on one of my front teeth. My brother, Jackie, who's three years younger than me, got the worst of the deal; he didn't get slapped around as much, but he was cursed with thoroughbred buckteeth. A couple of them were chipped too.

The old man's radiator shop was at the corner of Silva and Central streets in Pawtucket. It was a well-known landmark because of a once witty slogan the old man thought up and stamped all over the place, which I sometimes found embarrassing, like an old joke, and anyway not nearly as clever as the Rhode Island State Lottery ad which from the window proclaimed PICK A WINNER. The shop was called Pop's—the old man's nickname; he bragged that he'd earned the title "because I popped so many niggers when I was a boy." He'd grown up on Federal Hill in Providence, the only Irish kid in an Italian neighborhood. In the good old days he and his *paisans* would venture into South Providence on Saturday nights and beat the shit out of black guys. "Now," he said, "it's crazy, you could get yourself killed going into South Providence. They've let the place go to hell." For a long time my brother and I pretended to hate blacks. Figured we'd be fools not to. At some point, though, I realized that a lot of what the old man told me was bullshit. Like the time in first grade I asked him what the I.N.R.I. on the top of the crucifix stood for. He told me it meant "In Rhode Island."

When I was thirteen, my old man wasted the

family dog, Clops. It was inevitable. Clops liked to terrorize the neighborhood cats and had been identified as the cold-blooded savage who'd beheaded a local kitten. Later, when he was charged with ripping the jugular out of Mrs. Hanley's Siamese cat (in front of the Hanleys' horrified six-year-old daughter), the old man decided it was time.

My brother, Jackie, had found Clops down by the power lines two years earlier. The mangiest mutt I'd ever laid eyes on, he was the size of an emaciated fox and almost entirely bald except for blotches of fur scattered haphazardly on his body. He had only one eye and in the two years we knew him he never once used his right hind leg in our presence. Just let it hang there like an old man's limp pecker. But love is blind, and Jackie believed that Clops was some kind of runaway royal pedigree. He once woke me in the middle of the night worried that Clops might be dognapped and exploited as a show dog. "Look at him," he said. "How many dogs you know who can run on three legs?"

Right from the start the old man hated Clops's guts. Not

just the "You can't keep the mutt" kind of hatred but the "Let's put the fleabag to sleep" variety. Fortunately, Caveech loved dogs and said, "It'll teach the kids maturity."

"I'll get them a *real* mutt then," the old man said. "One with two eyes and four legs."

Eventually he gave in, and we were allowed to keep him. Because of the one eye, Jackie named him Cyclops and, thus, Clops.

I always figured that a heavyweight alley cat must have been the one to gouge out Clops's right eye because, despite it, he managed to ambush just about every cat in the neighborhood. Got so bad that I hung a big bell from his collar to tip the cats off, but it didn't do shit. Clops continued to limp home at least once or twice a month with bloody fur around his mouth. Then came the fateful day when he snatched the Hanleys' Siamese cat out of the loving hands of the little six-year-old. He was finished. A mob of hysterical neighbors came running over to the house, and Mr. Hanley shoved a bloodied clump of cat into my and Jackie's faces as if *we'd* killed the poor thing.

That night when the old man returned home from a Local 57 softball game, Mr. Hanley gave him a call and described what had happened. The old man's only words to the man were, "Don't worry. He's dead." With that he hung up the phone, glared at Jackie and me, and said, "Where's that bald-headed bag of dead cats?"

Neither of us answered.

"Well? Where is the little worm?"

"Outside," Jackie said.

The old man went to the front door and whistled. Clops ran up but, upon entering the old man's shadow, slammed on his leathery brakes and stopped. He turned his head to the side and looked at us. The old man reached for him but Clops jumped back and retreated to the sidewalk. My brother was ordered to call him.

"No," he said, "you're gonna hurt him."

The old man grabbed Jackie by his shirt and picked him up on his tippy-toes. "You call that goddamn mutt or I'm gonna hurt *you*. You know I could get sued for this?"

Jackie started crying. "Come here, Clops," he muttered.

The dog climbed back up the steps and stopped. I stood behind the old man and waved my hands over my head to warn Clops that it was a setup.

"Call him again," the old man said.

"Here, Clops," said Jackie.

With his tail limp, Clops started into the house. The old man slammed the door on the dog's neck and fell against it in a rage. Clops's eye bulged out of its socket. For thirty seconds the old man's face bubbled with blood as he grunted and pressed his 250 pounds against the door. Jackie ran out of the room, crying. I stayed. First noise I heard sounded like the sharp crack of pool balls on a good break. Several lesser snaps followed.

Finally the old man released his hold and Clops slumped to our welcome mat.

"I warned you to keep that fleabag away from cats!" the old man said. "You don't want to listen? This is what you get. Now go throw him in the river."

I picked Clops up and walked outside. He didn't move in my arms but I had a glimmer of hope that he was just playing dead.

"Make sure you heave him out far," the old man called. "I don't want no carcass washing up near here, *capisce?* He'll smell up the fucking town."

When I got out on the sidewalk, I put Clops down and examined him under a streetlight. He lay still, his good eye wide open. I heard little noises that sounded like his stomach growling. Reminded me that he hadn't been fed yet. I felt awful. I petted him to get him to wag his tail or something. Anything. Finally he whimpered so I figured he was going to make it. When the old man went to the bathroom, I snuck Clops back inside. Jackie stopped bawling when I slipped into the bedroom carrying his dog.

"Is he dead?" Jackie whispered.

"No," I said. "Gonna be okay, I think."

"We better hide him good. He's slunkmeat if Pop finds him up here."

Jackie and I slept in my bed with Clops tucked between us beneath the covers. I woke up at five in the morning and turned on a pen flashlight that I kept hidden between the mattresses. Flashed the light in Clops's face. His eye was open. Tried to stick my finger in his mouth to see if he was still warm, but his jaw was chilled shut. I pointed the light on Jackie. His arms were wrapped around his dead dog's head as if Clops were a teddy bear. A dab of blood had dripped out of Clops's mouth and stained Jackie's undershirt.

It was getting light out so I climbed out of bed and pulled on a pair of dungarees and a Boston Bruins jersey. I gently pried my brother's arms from around Clops's head. When I lifted the dog's body, Jackie woke up, startled.

"Take it easy," I said.

"What are you doing?"

I laid Clops on the floor and tied my sneakers.

"I'm taking Clops out to the country. Gonna give him away to a farmer. Now be quiet, I don't want him to wake up. He had a rough night."

"What if he don't want to stay out there?"

"He'll stay. He likes the outdoors."

Jackie wiped crusted saliva from his cheek. "Don't let Pop hear you. He'll have a conniption."

"Relax," I said, picking Clops's body up in my arms, "I got it under control."

As I walked out of the bedroom, Jackie whispered in an exaggerated falsetto, "Goodbye, Clopsy. I'll come visit you baby."

Once I got outside, I dropped the dog's starched body into a white canvas *Providence Journal* delivery bag and headed down the street with the bag over my shoulder. Clops was so stiff that all four of his legs stuck out of the bag. Even the limp pecker-leg was now a rigid hard-on.

I crossed the Junction Street Bridge and passed a grim row of window-blackened mills. The stale breath of the river gave way to the fumes of the highway. Climbed a hill and hopped a guardrail to get on Route 95. Pawtucket was experiencing a July heat wave, and by six o'clock the temperature was already in the low eighties. I'd been walking and thumbing for thirty minutes when two middle-aged Italian men in a white Impala stopped.

"How you doing, kid?" the man in the passenger seat asked as I got in.

"Good, thank you," I said.

He glanced at the legs sticking out of my bag but didn't show any reaction. "Where you going?"

"Cumberland."

"Well, we'll get you about halfway there, buddy."

We'd driven about a mile when the driver looked in his rearview mirror for the first time, did a quick double take, and glanced over his shoulder at Clops's legs. "Hey, kid," he said, "you know yooz got an animal in your bag?"

The passenger said, "No shit, Sherlock. It's the kid's dog, you pea brain."

The driver looked blankly at his friend and then peeked back at the dog feet. "I got some bad news for you," he said.

I caught his eye in the mirror and raised my eyebrows.

"I think your pooch is dead."

"You fucking banana," the passenger said. "You think the kid don't already *know* that?" He threw me a compassionate squint. "What happened? He get hit by a car?"

I looked out the window and said, "Yeah."

"Mind if I ask you a question?" the driver said. "How long you been carrying that corpse around with you?"

"Just this morning. Going to Cumberland to bury him."

"Why don't you just dump him in a trash can?"

The passenger told the driver to shut his trap and take me to wherever I was going. They turned off on Route 295 and drove me all the way to Cumberland. I thanked them and climbed out in front of a cornfield. Took me two hours to dig the grave with my hands. Just before I lowered Clops and the bag into the hole, I kissed his head. He didn't smell dead yet.

When I returned home at noon, Jackie wasn't around. I kicked around the city all afternoon looking for things to do.

But there was nothing. It was a doomed day. The air burnt my nostrils as it had the day I was chased by several boys through a tunnel at rush hour. The sun shone but the sky was a pale blue, almost gray. The chaos of car horns, children playing, and dogs barking made me sick to my stomach. My fingernails were caked with dirt.

Heard the news as the church bells were ringing at 6 P.M. Jackie'd been messing around and grabbed the wrong wire, that's all. The fluttery electrical charge wasn't enough to even burn his fingers, but it scared the shit out of him and he fell thirty feet off the power line. A paperboy found him lying beside one of the metal skeletons.

The doctors said it was a miracle that Jackie survived after the way he'd shattered the bones in his neck. I was grateful to whoever had the final say in whether or not to finish him off; there were conflicting reports. My grandmother cried, "It's the devil's work! It's the devil's work!" Twenty minutes later she said, "Why, God? Why did You do this?"

I was allowed to visit Jackie three days later. He was lying upside down in Rhode Island Hospital. Metal screws were drilled into his skull, but he said he felt great. When the old man left the room to speak with the doctors, Jackie asked me to make sure nobody was listening.

"You find any farms, Dunph?"

" 'Course," I said. I sat and turned my head so that I was looking up at him. "I saw this farm with about ten dogs out front so I asked the guy who lived there if he could use any more. You know, I explained the deal with the old man and all."

"And?"

"And he took him. You know, at first he said he already had too many dogs and he had a bunch of sheeps and stuff, too, so he thought it might be a problem feeding him and all. But, you know, I told him all about Clops eating cats and how he hardly wouldn't have to feed him at all. Then Clops comes running around the corner and, I'm telling you, the guy goes wild. Should've seen his eyes light up."

Jackie smiled, and I got carried away.

"He loved Clops right away. Said he was either gonna use him as a show dog or he might just keep him around the farm for fox hunts."

"Fox hunts?!"

"Yeah, he said Clops would be great as a fox-hunt dog. Looks so much like a fox he could probably blend right in and lead a whole family of dumbshit foxes right up to a bunch of hunters."

Jackie glowed. "I told you he was probably a show dog, didn't I?"

When visiting hours were over, a nurse handed me a plastic bag containing the clothes my brother had on when he got to the hospital. At home I emptied it out and saw that Jackie had been wearing the same stained undershirt that he'd worn when he slept with me and Clops, but the blood from Clops's mouth had dried and looked like chocolate.

I was introduced to Suicide by Joey DeCenzo and Mousy Town. Suicide was the steepest hill in Pawtucket. When it snowed, the guys who hung out there would slide down it on toboggans. Madness. Once you got going there was no stopping. You just had to pray that nothing would run you over at the bottom. In the sixties, two kids riding on the same toboggan had been flattened by a sanding truck; everyone was hooked. It became a test of courage called Rhode Island Roulette.

I never rode on a toboggan with DeCenz. No sane person would. I've seen him break a leg jumping off a sixty-foot-high trestle into a shallow section of the Blackstone River—just to see if it could be done without breaking a leg. Another time, at a party, DeCenz stood against a wall and allowed Drugs Delaney to throw darts around his head from fifteen feet. Didn't even blink until he got drilled in the chin.

But DeCenz wasn't your standard Pawtucket sicko. Although he was six feet four, covered with body hair, and 230 pounds by the time he was fifteen, he was a harmless beast. One time, five or six of us were hanging out throwing snowballs when this pissed-off gearhead with a wad of snow in his ear suddenly slammed on his brakes and came charging us on foot clutching a baseball bat. Nobody budged. Wasn't as if we'd been throwing grenades. When the guy was halfway across the street he had to realize he'd made a grave miscalculation, but it looked as if he'd made a graver one when he went after the biggest kid in an obvious attempt to intimidate us. He raised the Louisville Slugger and took a mighty swing at DeCenz, actually cracking the bat over his shoulder. Anyone else would have been organ-donor material. There was electricity in the air while everyone waited for DeCenz's reaction. When the crowd sensed mercy, they started yelling for the terrified gearhead's scalp. DeCenz massaged his shoulder and said, "Hey, chicken-neck, are you fucking nuts?" To everyone's disappointment, though, he just carried the gearhead back to his jacked-up Chevy and stuffed him in through the open window. The guy squealed away looking more confused than if he'd been pummeled. But that's the way DeCenz was; he wasn't out to hurt anyone but himself.

Mousy Town told him he might as well—hurt himself—because we were facing an early death in the coming nuclear holocaust anyway. Most of the Suicide Hillers bought this. There were so many signs. The bear and the eagle, the Nicaraguan earthquake, all the volcanoes everywhere. Wars, famine, the Middle East. Mousy said that the nostalgia revival was merely mankind's life flashing before its eyes. And, the kicker—Haley's Comet was coming back around. He could practically hear the fuse fizzling in the distance. Which I believe now, seeing as Mousy would die so young.

Drugs Delaney disagreed. We were doomed all right, but it was because earth was going to collide with a mammoth meteorite sometime in early 1978. His cousin had received this hot tip from one of his teachers at "Reject"—that's how everyone pronounced R.I.J.C.—which stood for Rhode Island Junior College. "They ain't telling us though," Drugs said, " 'cause if everyone knew then what would stop guys from grabbing every girl's tit that they passed on the street?"

The old man and Caveech hated Mousy's guts. They called him "Spinach Chin" because of his beard. Caveech said, "All guys with fuzzy pusses are closet queens. That's why they grow it. They're afraid they look too much like broads."

"What about Abe Lincoln?" I said.

"As queer as they come," Caveech said.

Nunzio Cavichhi had been the old man's *paisan* since they

were child hoods. Caveech was as loud, definitely as bigoted, equally irked about life, but far more blubbery. At five foot eight he jolted the scales at 400 pounds, although he claimed he was only flirting with "three and a half yards." Caveech was bald and his face slick and shiny. Deep folds around his mouth gave his jaw a puppety look. I never knew exactly what he did for a living, but he always did it in a three-piece suit. There was such a strain on his vest buttons that I figured they were sewn on with fishing line.

I didn't try to defend Mousy from Caveech and the old man. I knew they were just pissed off that I was spending all my time on Suicide. Practically every night I got drunk at the Hilltop Cafe (fifteen cents a draught) and then I climbed a water tower. The drinking age in Rhody was eighteen, but it wasn't strictly enforced in Pawtucket and pubic monsters like DeCenz and Mousy had been getting served since they were thirteen. The 240-foot-high cylindrical water tower on Suicide jutted skyward like a buoy in a sea of lights. Late at night we climbed it and peaked over the murk.

The old man called me a fruit for growing my hair long— even though I reluctantly kept it parted on the side—and he hated me for coming home drunk or stoned and for letting my schoolwork shit the bed. But I don't think the old man seriously considered Caveech's offer to pull some strings and get me a free ride to boarding school until the maple tree incident.

It was almost two in the morning when Mousy, DeCenz, and I drove past the great, scarred tree that two city employees were preparing to butcher. Mousy pulled the car over and looked back at them. "That's a crock of shit if ever I saw one," he said.

I wasn't surprised. The maple tree had gained notoriety when one of the mayor's right-hand men had been discovered sleeping and bleeding against it in a wrinkled Caddy at five o'clock on New Year's morning. In the week since, the tree had been accused of everything except failing to submit to a breathalizer test. The right-hand man got off scot-free, and the hundred-year-old maple was sentenced to be amputated from the earth while the city slept.

Mousy squeezed the steering wheel. "Check out that shit."

DeCenz and I watched out the back window through a cloud of exhaust.

"Think about it," Mousy said. "That makes about as much sense as knocking down the Golden Gate Bridge just to keep loonies from jumping off it."

"Yeah," DeCenz said, "but that's a bad corner to have a tree."

"A bad corner to have a tree? Come off it, DeCenz, it's a bad corner to have a corner. The tree ain't in the road. If anything, they could pull the road over on the other side."

"They'd have to knock down the building," I said, pointing out the warehouse across the street.

"So?"

"Guess they don't own it," I said.

"But they own the tree?"

"Guess so."

"Boy, whoever programmed you guys sure knew what he was doing."

"Just goes to show you," DeCenz said, "you can't fight city hall."

"Bullshit," Mousy said, "that's the problem with this place, the people are pussies. They'll eat any shit the city feeds them. You're wrong, DeCenz, we're the *only* ones who can fight them . . . because we're the only ones who care."

When the old man picked me up at the pig station the next morning, he showed a lot of restraint. He did call me "jailbird" a couple times on the way home and suggested I thank Caveech that no charges were pressed, but he kept his fists clamped to the steering wheel. He asked what we'd intended by linking arms and wrapping ourselves around a tree.

"We were trying to stop them from chopping it down."

"What, you got Grapenuts for brains? You truly thought that would stop them? 'Oh, gee whiz, we didn't know that you fellas liked this tree. We'll just go home and explain to the mayor in the morning.' Sometimes you think like a goddamn Portagee!"

He was right about it being a futile cause. The two executioners had had the tree half-carved before the oinkers were finished interrogating us at the scene.

"It was the symbolism of the act," I said weakly.

"Symbolism? Well symbolism this, Dildo. That was your last performance as a Rhode Island high school student. Huh, symbolism."

The next day he handed me a brochure for a Protestant Episcopal prep school called Cornwall Academy. "Here," he said, "read about your new home. If things go good, you're gonna be moving in next week." C.A. described itself as "an exemplary private educational institution founded in 1845 and located in Cornwall, Connecticut." It had "opened its doors to meritorious young women in 1958" but employed one of the surest contraceptives known to man: the girls' dorms were located six miles from the boys'. It was started by the Boston-born theologian Theodore Coolidge and was "designed to inculcate morals in the world's future leaders."

The old man pointed to "inculcate" and said, "Look at that, Dildo. Tell me they don't know what they're talking about."

A dog's asshole is cleaner than a human tongue. That's what DeCenz said. It was January 17, 1974, the night before I was sent to Cornwall and he, Tommy the Wire, Mousy, and I were on the water tower getting stoned. (Drugs Delaney never trusted himself enough to climb the tower.)

"No way," I said.

"I shit you not," DeCenz said. "It's a fact that it has less germs."

"What about a rat's ass?" the Wire asked.

"Don't know," said DeCenz. "Think it's probably dirtier than a dog's."

"Yeah," the Wire said, "but is it cleaner than your tongue?"

DeCenz didn't know for sure.

"Did you read about the poor sucker who got charged with murder for pulling the plug on his brother who was in an iron lung?" Mousy asked.

"Insurance scam?" the Wire said.

"Nah. The guy's in this iron lung, totally paralyzed; he can't talk, he can't breathe on his own, can't even open his eyes. He's got tubes around his cock, up his ass; the poor guy's a mess. So his brother comes to see him one day, and he figures he'd be better off dead. You got to understand that this is his *bro.* He knew they were just torturing his mind by keeping him alive. So he pulled the plug."

"And they charged him with murder?" I asked.

"He better of got charged!" Tommy the Wire said. "I mean, everybody could start saying that. That's all I need. My sleazy brother would be snaking his way into the hospital first chance he got. What a joke. Believe me, nobody wants to die."

"*I* would if I was like that," Mousy said.

"Me too," DeCenz added.

"Well, yooz guys is fucked then," the Wire said, successfully pulling the plug on the discussion.

Later, after we'd dropped Tommy the Wire off, Mousy brought it up again. "Seriously," he said, "if I ever remotely resemble that guy's brother, I hope you'd have the decency to put me out of my misery. I mean, you'd just be finishing off God's work."

DeCenz and I nodded. We drove several blocks.

"How bad would you have to be?" DeCenz finally asked.

Mousy didn't answer at first. When we stopped at a red light, he said, "I don't know. Guess I'd have to be so bad that my life obviously wasn't worth living. I think you'd just know."

There wasn't much of a scene at the train station the next day. Jackie was home from the clinic, and he waited on the platform with me. The old man had given me thirty dollars and a one-way ticket.

"Look, Dildo," the old man said. "I'm doing this for your own fucking good."

I was very pissed-off, though, and didn't answer.

"Hey, don't give me that look," he said. "My old man would've sent me to one of these joints, too, if he could've swung it. You know why? Because you're gonna get a damn good education about people."

Just before the train left, Jackie pulled out this grandfather clock of a wristwatch that he'd scored off Caveech. Must've weighed five pounds and gave the time in about ten different countries. It was some kind of scuba diver's watch with a compass, an alarm, and a calendar; it played a tune and even contained a little foldable toothpick. Jackie said it was worth two hundred dollars, but Caveech had gotten him a bargain and it only cost $7.50.

"That's some bargain," I said. "I'm surprised it don't come with its own wrist."

"You're welcome," he said, and I thanked him.

There was a loud, painful hiss, and the train jerked forward. I hopped aboard, immediately regretting not having hugged my brother. Jackie rolled along beneath my window until we got to the end of the platform, and I left him behind.

PART *Two*

January is a cold month in western Connecticut. Especially when you're living in a crumbling dormitory during the oil crisis at a school that apparently didn't fund-raise well. I froze my grapes off. Mornings were brutal. As I scurried down the echoey hall toward a breakfast of powdered eggs and a chilly slice of toast, I felt as if my body had emptied of blood. I never felt comfortable until I was standing in the shower; then just when I'd begin to thaw out, I'd get pushed out into the drafty lavatory. Nights were worse. Two of the windowpanes in my room were broken, and the little warmth that managed to clank out of my radiator was sucked into the night and disappeared in a puff of smoke.

Fortunately, I met Billy-Fu Sodani. He was the son of a Pakistani oil minister whose wealth was estimated in the quarter-billion-dollar range. He was also the biggest drug dealer on campus. Billy-Fu didn't deal for the money, but for the risk involved. Like those people who parachute just because it scares the turds out of them. Adventure being discomfort in retrospect and all that. His real name was Fuad, but he always wore a cowboy hat and he'd gotten this nickname.

A few nights a week Billy-Fu and I would stuff our beds and sneak out of the dorms. We'd scamper across campus, darting between every bush. A quick dash up the side of the mountain, and we were ready to get high. Even at that point, though, things weren't exactly what Billy-Fu called "copacetic." Besides freezing our fingers off trying to light the bowl, there was the possibility of being ambushed by a swarm of teachers. The school encouraged this as part of its "administrative pervasion."

Kids were getting bounced from school three and four at a time. One guy actually went gray and then bald in the three days between his getting busted for dealing a few lids and facing the Disciplinary Committee for sentencing. Everyone thought he had a bad case of cancer or something. After he got booted, he went home to his doctor and they figured out that when his room was raided his heart must've actually stopped for a split second, long enough for all the hair on his body to wither.

Smoking dope or drinking were the easiest ways to get the boot, but even lighting a candle in your room could get you twelve hours labor because matches were contraband. Tension gripped the dorms like the ice outside. Knocking unannounced freaked people out. Bongs spilt on bedspreads, lit cigarettes were flung out windows, those already on probation hung from their fingertips from third-floor ledges, those on double-pro *dropped* from third-floor ledges, random drugs were gobbled down, and so on. The standard procedure was to knock and say "cool" simultaneously. Only teachers knocked without "cooling."

Students spoke of those expelled as if they were all dead. As far as the Academy was concerned, they were. Once dismissed, you had twelve hours to get lost and you were forevermore *persona non grata.*

I was walking down the boardwalk after I'd been at Cornwall about two weeks when a large bandaged paw reached out of Dean Mort's office and grabbed my arm.

"I've been searching for you, Mr. Dunphy," the Dean said.

"You have?" I asked nervously as he led me into his office.

"Yes, I have. Ever since I received this poignant note from a friend of yours called Drugs." He held an envelope away from his body as if it stunk.

"Drugs *Delaney?*"

"Mr. Dunphy, how many individuals named *Drugs* could you possibly associate with?"

"Just one, I guess."

"Then I suspect Drugs Delaney is our man."

I didn't get it. Dean Mort explained. Drugs had written a letter and forgot to put my name on the envelope. It was simply addressed to Cornwall Academy, Cornwall, Connecticut, and it had found its way to the Dean pretty quickly.

"Perhaps you'd better sit down," he said.

I did.

Then he began to read the letter aloud.

Greetings Dunph—

Whats happening? I got your letter today. Cornhole Academy sounds like it really sucks the big one. I can't believe they make everyone work a lot and not smoke. You should tell the head dick to shove it, you didn't want to go there in the first place. He'd shit!

Man, you shoulda seen me and Costa today at school today. We got cocked on a pint of blackberry brandy and ate some T.H.C. on the bus. We were fucked! This teacher Mr. Rivera goes what's wrong with you Delaney because I kept laughing, so I go I'm fucked man! Everybody laughed like a bastard!

Hey, you should see this song I'm listening to. It's called Don't Bogart That Joint My Friend. I think its by a group called

(At this point a line slashed across Drugs's letter. There was a gap, and the letter continued farther down the page.)

This is a couple hours later. Must've nodded out, man. Now I think I don't remember the group neither. I think its a group. Hey, I gotta go because I'll probably definitely nod again. Tell me when your coming home. I'll get some shit for everyone and we'll go wild. You want me to send you any squeef or you got enough? Good luck not getting caught.

Cocked in R.I.—
Drugs

P.S.—Did you know that a dog's asshole is cleaner than a human bean's tongue?

I don't remember much of what the Dean said in the twenty minutes that he lectured me following the reading. I do remember that I kept putting my head between my legs, which I'm sure the Dean interpreted as a show of shame but was really an attempt to keep from passing out. Just before I left his office, Mort returned the letter to me. "I'm going to be honest with you, Dunphy," he said. "I didn't want you here in the first place." He pointed at me with his bandaged hand. "I know your type. You won't make it. However, as far as your slate here goes, I consider you clean. I don't care how much dope or booze you've had in the past, I'll treat you like everyone else until you show me otherwise. But, of course, you *will* show me otherwise."

For the first few weeks at Cornwall, all I could think about was my brother. Jackie had come home six months after his accident with a wheelchair and a few railroad tracks running down his back. We stayed in and read magazines about the outdoors. At night we listened to the Boston or Providence College teams on the radio. It's not that our house had suddenly become a luau, it's just that the city was a nightmare. The people, the weather, the sidewalks, the traffic—it wasn't a good place for a kid in a wheelchair.

By the next fall we'd started getting out a day or two each week. On Saturdays we had a job packing donations at the Salvation Army bin near the old man's shop. We'd been getting our stuff there free for years so we did it for nothing. And each Sunday that the Patriots had a home game we'd pack a lunch and a radio and thumb twenty miles up Route 1 to Schaefer Stadium.

You'd be amazed how difficult that is. Thumbing with someone in a wheelchair, I mean. I guess most people either didn't want to deal with getting the chair into their car or they were afraid he was going to piss all over the place. The first couple times Jackie felt bad for himself and said it was probably his fault that cars weren't stopping. "You're crazy," I told him, "it's *definitely* your fault."

Whenever there were a lot of empty seats the security guards let us right into the stadium. Usually, though, we sat in the parking lot and listened to the game on my brother's transistor radio. Jackie loved hearing the roar of the crowd when there was a big play.

In the spring we decided to be farmers. Since there wasn't any farmland nearby we were content to barber our eight-by-six-foot front yard. We planted shrubs, tomatoes, corn, pumpkins, and watermelons. Our watermelons ended up looking like small green peppers and our tomatoes like grapes, but it wasn't due to any sloth on our part. We were early-risers, dedicated farmers springing out into our quiet barnyard to give the rooster a kick. Jackie would wake me in the dark each morning with a glass of Carnation Instant Breakfast. "Come on, Dunph," he'd say, "you better down some mud." The reason we couldn't grow any country-fair-calibre vegetables was partly because the Blackstone's chemical-saturated banks bleached the juice out of them but also because the billboard on top of our house blocked the sun for most of the day. The old man would shake his head when he'd see us out front.

In July we won a settlement from the power company; they agreed to pay for Jackie's rehabilitation. Because Jackie had developed a breathing problem, the doctors said he'd be better off recuperating in Arizona. After he left, I let the garden slip a little. One day I came home and the old man had chopped down all the plants. I asked him why he did it, and he said, "Because it's stupid."

When Jackie had been sent away I'd missed him a lot but not nearly as much as I did when I got to Cornwall. Lying in bed one night, it started getting to me. I asked my roommate, Irving Waltham, if I could turn on his stereo to help take my mind off things.

"Absolutely not," he said from the bunk below me. "You know the rules. Lights and stereos are to be terminated at 10:30 sharp."

"Why do you have the thing then?" I said. "The speakers take up half the room, it's got more lights on it than Mission Control Houston, and you don't even listen to it during the best time of the day."

"I didn't make the rules."

I knew I wouldn't sleep until I spoke with Jackie but I'd have to call the old man to get his number. I had such a lump in my throat that I could hardly breathe. My short, quick gasps became loud enough for Irving to hear. "You all right up there?" he said.

I was afraid if I tried to answer I might break down completely, so I just dropped a thumbs-up sign. The room was dark, and Irving didn't see it.

"Are you okay, Dunphy?"

I jumped down from my bed. "Got to make a phone call," I said.

"You can't use the phones until morning."

"They turn them off at night?"

"No, but you're not supposed to be out of your room after 10:00."

As I was leaving, Irving called out, "I'm not going to lie for you if there's a bed check!"

After weaving around the bushes, hiding in the grid shadows of catwalks, and ducking between parked cars, I finally reached the phone room and slid into a graffiti-scarred booth. The cold air made me more composed, articulate. I called home collect.

"Tim *Dunphy?*" the old man asked the operator.

"Yeah," I said, checking the phone room entrance.

There was a moment of silence.

"Come on, Dildo, what the fuck. It's 11:30, you know I got work tomorrow."

"Please just get—"

"Do you accept the call?" interrupted the operator.

"No," he said. "Not at this hour."

On the way back I was spotted by a teacher and stung three hours for being out of my room after lights. When I tried to explain I got two more for insubordination, and when I asked the guy why he was being such a prick I was looking at a total of ten hours. That meant five straight afternoons working after class.

The next day I reported to the hour board at 3:15. Irving Waltham was working off hours, too. Fundy had us shovel snow and chip ice off the walks. "Fundy" was the head of the Hour Department. His real name was Bernard Funderburk, and he also taught history and political science. He was around twenty-five years old with a baby face and an erratically balding lid. He fought it though, pulling his overgrown left sideburn all the way over his head. Fundy took his job seriously. "You work two hours a day," he said, "and if I catch you resting once, they don't count."

As soon as Fundy left to go check up on another crew of

hour-boys, a few kids started getting on Irving's case. You see, Irving Waltham was a jellyfish. He was shy and unassuming, with Coke-bottle-glasses taped up in the corners with Band-Aids. A couple of inches of pale shin showed between his pants and his socks. His hair was cemented back with something shiny, and he wore a fluorescent-orange hunter's cap. It wasn't like he was real soft or anything—he was actually kind of scrappy-looking—but what a pussy.

"Look pissed," I said. "It'll scare them off."

A snowball exploded off the back of his head, but he kept shoveling. "It doesn't work. That's just giving them what they want."

"What do they want?"

"They want me to get mad."

"Then why aren't they throwing at me? I'd get very mad."

Irving didn't answer. A snowball whizzed past his head.

"Just give them a dirty look or something," I said.

"Leave me alone."

I began chipping ice down the walk in a different direction than Waltham. When I was about twenty feet from him, I heard a loud "clack," a moan, and I turned in time to see Irving's glasses skate across the sidewalk. He dropped his shovel and knelt in the snow, covering his right eye. The hour-boys continued shoveling. I picked up his glasses. The lenses were scratched, and one of the earpieces had broken off.

"You okay?" I asked.

Irving didn't look up. I thought he might be crying.

"Did it hit you in the eye?"

He faced me. "What do you think?"

There was something about seeing him without his glasses

on that was pathetic. His injured eye was partially closed and already a little black-and-blue. I tried to fix his glasses but the Band-Aid wouldn't stick any more. Irving grabbed them from me.

"The thing fell off," I said.

He put them in his coat pocket. I went to pick up his hat, and he said, "Just leave it alone." I picked it up anyway and gave it to him.

"You know why they don't throw at you?" he said. "Because you're one of them. They can sense it."

"Come on, Irv. I was just trying to help—"

"I don't need your help! If it weren't for you, I wouldn't even be here."

I went back to chipping. Ten minutes later it finally occurred to me. I worked my way back to Irving.

"How's the eye?" I said.

"Great."

"Listen, I appreciate your covering for me last night if that's why you're here."

Irving kept shoveling.

"That was nice," I said.

"That's all right. You probably would've done the same for me."

"You're right," I said, "I would've. And I'm with you now if you want to bean the bastard who hit you in the eye."

"Thanks. But I really don't want to."

"That's cool," I said.

Irving and I lived in the Dining Hall dorm. Mr.
Funderburk also lived on our floor. At the beginning of the
trimester I discovered a family of mice living in the walls.
Practically every day I'd come face to face with one of them.
They weren't very big—two inches at most—but they had
Fundy a nervous wreck.

He had his hour-boys spread rat poison throughout the
buildings at both the Boys and Girls Schools. One day I found
one of the mice lying in the hallway, completely gassed. Wasn't
dead but he wasn't too alive either. Later I found two more
lying on my bedroom floor and another under a radiator in the
bathroom. I couldn't tell how long they'd hang on, but I wasn't
about to pull out a stopwatch either. While everyone was at
dinner, I grabbed a hockey stick out of my neighbor's closet,
stickhandled the mice out into the hall, and quickly clobbered
the shit out of them. The following week I wasted at least ten
more. Funderburk was pissed off. He wanted to know who'd
messed up the hallway.

I decided to get even. On the last day I was working off
hours, I snuck into the dorm. No one was around. I held a
lighter under Fundy's doorknob for a good five minutes, all the
time looking out the window at the end of the hall, waiting for
him to come by on his rounds. When the metal doorknob was
practically glowing and I could barely hold onto the lighter,
along came Fundy. I stood back from the window so he
couldn't see me, and yelled, "Fire in Funderburk's room!"
Then I slipped down a rear stairwell and got back to work.

Fundy ran to his apartment, seared his hand on the doorknob, and panicking, dashed from the dorm pulling every fire alarm in sight. By the time the fire department arrived, the doorknob was as cool as a cucumber and Fundy looked like a little fruitcake. That perked me up for a few days.

Occasionally I hung out with a kid

from Greenwich, Connecticut, named Jonathan Wheeler. Wheeler got along better with girls than with guys. Mousy had warned me that kids like that are either queers or back stabbers. In any case, he was very popular up at the Girls School. I doubt he would've been, though, if the girls knew that he referred to them as "cracks." (A girlfriend was a "main crack," his grandmother was his "grandcrack," and so on.)

Wheeler started chasing a flashy Scarsdale debutante named S.D. (Sydney Deavenworth) Stuart. She was his "dream crack." One day he showed up in my room with big plans. The following Sunday, he said, S.D., himself, me, and another girl were to have lunch in town at a fancy restaurant that had the "chunkiest bleu cheese dressing in Connecticut." (The kid wasn't stupid; he knew I wouldn't be able to afford anything but the salad bar.)

"Who's the other girl?" I asked.

"Good friend of S.D.'s."

"What does she look like?"

"Let me put it this way, Dunphy: She's the face that launched a thousand lunches." Wheeler broke up.

"Hideous?"

"Fair to partly hideous. And somewhat huge."

"What's her name?"

"Ogre Penderghastly."

Her real name was Olga Pendergast, and she was in my French class. She was a pretty friendly kid and not nearly as horrible as Wheeler described, but she'd acquired this awful alias, partly because her real name invited it, but mostly, I guess, because she almost always wore a pair of spotless painter's pants that were several sizes too small and made a spectacle of her already ample ass. Olga was a shameless preppy, one of those lime-green-sweater-crocodile-shirt-boat-shoe clones who think everything's "tacky" except old Frank Sinatra albums, Head-of-the-Charles races, smores, and *Mack the Knife*. But, like I said, she was friendly.

"Friendly?" Wheeler said. "Come off it, Dunphy, the girl's a rhino. She's *got* to be friendly."

"You trying to talk me out of this?"

"No way. Let's face it, Carrot Top, you ain't no box of chocolates yourself."

It hurt to hear it spelled out like that, but it *had* been a long time since I'd been with a girl. He was right: It was beast or famine.

Wheeler phoned the girls Sunday morning and told them we'd meet in town and then walk to the restaurant. At the 10 o'clock chapel service I prayed to God and all my dead relatives that Olga would wear a skirt. Well, if there's a God, I'm sure he's got bigger fish to fry, so I couldn't really complain when Olga showed up jammed into her painter's pants. She was also blessed with a flowering boil on her chin, which she soon rubbed into full bloom.

At the restaurant Wheeler started reminiscing about all the delicacies in the various countries he'd toured with his father. S.D. and Olga had seen their share of foreign soil so they kept right up with him.

Jonathan convinced them to try an Indian appetizer, which he said, along with the bleu cheese dressing, the restaurant was famous for. I swear they were called Indian Chicken Balls. They were yellow, doughy things about the size of a Ping-Pong ball and were sprinkled with coconut. I was dying to try one, but I didn't want to beg and they each ate the three they were served.

Wheeler told us all about his trip to India and how everyone's either rich or starving and practically everything they serve has coconut on it and so on. After the chicken balls, they each had a cup of some kind of cold soup. Then came a dozen cooked clams with bacon and cheese melted all over them. My stomach felt as if it would cave in if I didn't eat soon so when S.D. offered me a clam I grabbed the biggest one and started chomping. But the more I chomped, the bigger it got. Before I knew it, I had a mouthful of clam too large to swallow and my jaw was starting to ache. I tried to break it into smaller pieces but I've got flat teeth I guess and I couldn't get through it. It had the texture and taste of cardboard. All right, I thought, don't panic. Spit it into your napkin when nobody's looking. Unfortunately, Olga was in the midst of a ten-minute sour-grapes-iloquy about her ex-boyfriend and was looking me straight in the eye. Just when nausea started to set in, she glanced down at her plate. Pthew. The paper napkin went to my mouth, and I gripped the chaw of clam. I rolled the napkin into a ball and put it in the ashtray.

During the rest of the meal the girls kept peppering me

with questions about my old high school. What were the differences between a public high and a prep school? There were many, I said, most of them simply relating to the sizes of the two. Cornwall had about six hundred students and my old high school had close to three thousand.

I told them about the time I was sleeping through an English class in tenth grade. There were about fifty kids in this room, and everybody was always going wild so I used to just lay my head on my desk and nod out. One day while I was snoozing, I suddenly heard the teacher call out my name. I snapped to attention and looked around in a stupor, figuring I was in some kind of shit. But the teacher didn't say anything. After class someone told me that she'd actually been using me as an example of a "good" student. Everyone had been making such a racket that she'd yelled out, "Why can't you all just be like Mr. Dunphy and leave me alone!"

All in all the lunch went pretty smoothly until Olga noticed a lipstick mark on her water glass. It was her own lipstick but she thought it looked gross and searched for something to wipe it off with. Before I could stop her, she grabbed the folded-up ball of napkin out of the ashtray and started wiping her glass. The wad of toothmarks plopped onto the table and Olga screamed.

"My God, what is it?" S.D. said.

"This place is disgusting," I said.

"This place?" said Wheeler. "You're the disgusting one, Dunphy. That was *your* napkin."

After that I felt sort of out of it for the rest of the afternoon and in a way, I guess, that's how I felt for those first two months.

I thumbed home to Pawtucket for March vacation and went straight to the Hilltop Cafe. The Hilltop was a tiny stone building with a faded Narragansett beer sign out front. Dusty, stuffed fish were nailed to the knotty-pine walls inside, and a broken pinball machine covered with forgotten bowling trophies was jammed into the corner. Pickled eggs and pigs' feet sat in big jars behind the bar. The place reeked of cigarettes and beer mingling with the faint odor of stuffed-up shitters.

Mousy was the first person I saw. We stood over a tense, paycheck-potted pitch game. DeCenz, Drugs Delaney, and Tommy the Wire watched me from across the room. They were pissed off at me for not giving the old man a harder time about sending me to Cornwall.

"Oh, Jeez," the Wire finally called, "look who just flown in. Mr. Snuffington. You catch a limo from the airport?"

"What a sport," DeCenz said. "He's come home to visit his cronies."

"Shut up, you guys," Mousy said. "I don't blame you, Dunph, I would've went, too."

Mousy and I moved to the booth with the other guys and drank dollar-twenty-five-cent pitchers of beer. It was Friday night, and they were a quarter off. I bragged that I'd learned how to play backgammon, and Tommy the Wire said, "Backgammon this."

After our fourth pitcher we were speculating about what

we'd do with our lives. Drugs Delaney was lucky. He knew his calling.

"Reefer, man," he said. "They're gonna have to legalize it in five years, and then no one but the conglomities are gonna make out. The government has millions of acres of reefer growing underground in Alaska right now, man. Don't believe all that pipeline shit; they're just planting a lot of grass and they're waiting for the day it's legalized. My cousin read about it in some top-secret CIA stuff that a friend of his stole when he was working for the post office last summer. Like they have these wicked modern underground greenhouses just full of the shit for when they legalize it. That's no shit, man. Till then, I'm gonna be doing my own selling. And not just LBs, man. Talking tons. As soon as I get enough money to buy a boat, I'm gonna clean up."

We were divided on the best time to settle down. Drugs thought that twenty-five was a good age to get married "as long as your old lady's twenty-one or younger." Tommy the Wire said he'd wait until he was thirty-five and then marry a twenty-one-year-old. "That way," he said, "when you're fifty, she'll only be thirty-one. And by the time she starts getting real nasty, with the knotty legs and all, you'll either be planted or you won't be able to get it up no more anyhow."

"You're both crazy," DeCenz said. "You marry a twenty-one-year-old chick when you're twenty-five. Then when you're thirty-five and she's thirty-one, you become a Mormon and marry another twenty-one-year-old."

"Who wants to be a Mormon?" the Wire asked.

"You kidding?" DeCenz said. "Those guys have like fifty wives each. And they're fucking hot."

After the Hilltop closed, Mousy, DeCenz, the Wire, and I climbed the water tower. "I'm sick of the East Coast," Mousy said. "It's too damn crowded and, what the hell, just because I was born here don't mean I gotta stay. I'm thinking of heading out West."

"What's wrong with Pawtucket?" Tommy the Wire asked.

"Sick of it," Mousy said. "It's taking me nowhere, real slow. Just look at all the people who commit side-sui around here."

"Where?" the Wire asked, indignant.

"Here," Mousy said, "all over the East." He lit a butt. DeCenz looked at me. (Of my friends, only he and Mousy knew about my mother.)

"Oh, cut the shit," the Wire said. "You'd have to be a fucking fruitcake to even consider side-sui."

"You'd be surprised," Mousy said. "Anyone could do it. *I* could. Too much pressure, too little fresh air, too little time. I don't like taking orders, and I ain't gonna sell out. A couple years I'll be twenty and then thirty, and," he paused, "that could be it."

Mousy was referring to a pledge he'd made that when he turned thirty he was going to scrutinize his life and, should he not approve of what he saw, it was going to be el leapo from the nearest unoccupied water tower. Called it "beating the bombs." We always got a kick out of him when he spoke of this event because his eyeballs would bulge, his tongue would hang, and then he'd stretch out his arms and turn them in a circular motion as if falling to his death.

"Gonna be clean living, early to bed and early to rise,"

Mousy said. "You can drink right out of the streams and rivers in some of those west states, you know."

DeCenz said, "Sounds nice. No smog, no black snow, no oil distilleries."

"Fuck no," Mousy said. "Just fresh air, mountains, trees, and lots of clean snow. You can avoid being a statistic out there."

"That's a crock of shit," the Wire yelled out. "Yooz guys seen *Jeremiah Johnson* too fucking much." He was drunk, his eyes a web of red, and when he got this way his neck was the same color. "You can't just quit life and move out West like goddamn hippies. Everyone's got to be a stat sometime."

"Don't be ignorant," Mousy said. *"That's* a crock of shit. You're just afraid to make a move. It's been like this all through history. Look at the morons who fought for the British during the American Revolution. What, you think they were all just brave beyond reason? Uh-uh. But they'd march straight into battle *knowing* that they were bullet catchers . . . dart boards . . . *coffin fillers.* And you better believe they were leaving a trail of British turds every step of the way. But, like fools, they strode forward. Why?"

"Because they were dumbshits?" DeCenz guessed.

"Because they'd been brainwashed into believing there was no other choice. But there was. And there still is, you guys!"

"I would've fought'n if I lived back then, too," Tommy the Wire said.

"Big deal," Mousy said. "You wouldn't have had tiddly-squat to lose anyway. You could've strolled up to the front line without even getting shot at."

"Why?" the Wire said. " 'Cause I'm quicker'n them?"

"No, moron. Because they never would've seen the whites of your eyes."

That was a pretty good one and DeCenz and I laughed.

"Come on, you guys," Mousy said, "open your eyes. *We're* on the front line. And we're all marching toward cancers and ulcers and alcoholism and heartache and then fucking death. Let's get out, huh. I mean it, Dunph. You happy here, or what?"

I shrugged.

"DeCenz, are your parents happy?" Mousy asked. "Is even one of your *grandparents* happy?"

"Not really," DeCenz said. "My grandparents are all dead. Remember I told you about my grammy who got creamed by the bus? She was the last one."

"Rough way to go," I said.

"Not really. She never knew what hit her."

"How do you know?" the Wire asked.

"Pigs said so."

"And you believe them?" the Wire said with a laugh. "Boy, are you fucking stupid. What do you think they're gonna say? That your fucking grammy was wide awake and scared shitless and knew she was about to croak?"

"Hey, fuck off," DeCenz said.

By the end of the night DeCenz and I agreed with Mousy. We had to get away from Pawtucket. Wire said that he'd "been borned" in Pawtucket so he should "croak" there, too.

Mousy, DeCenz, and I stood on the water tower, clasped our hands over our heads, and vowed to move to Arizona in June, 1975, right after we graduated. Tommy the Wire sat beside us, dangling his ripped sneakers from the tower, happily inhaling the city's late-night breath of bus fumes and factory spew, as we capped our vows by singing an old Kinks' song:

> I don't want to live
> in the city no more.
> I don't want to die
> in a nuclear war.
> I just want to move
> to a faraway shore.
> And live like an Ape man.

Mousy was happy when he dropped me and DeCenz off in front of my house. It's the last time I remember him that way. DeCenz and I sat on my steps and smoked a bone. For a while neither of us spoke. Then DeCenz got stoned.

"Dunph," he said.

"Mmm?"

"Did you know that if you stretched out your intestines they'd reach the moon?"

"What?"

"If you cut someone open and stretched out their intestines, they'd reach the moon."

"No shit?"

"It's a fact. Human intestines go on forever."

"Wow."

We stared at the moon.

"Hold it," I said. "You mean to tell me that it's a couple hundred thousand miles from my mouth to my asshole?"

"Yeah. That's why shit looks so bad."

"Wow," I said, and looked back up at the moon.

"Dunph," DeCenz said a few minutes later.

"Mmm?"

"How come you never talk about your old lady?"

"What?"

"Why don't you never talk about your mother?"

"Same reason no one else does; she's dead."

He nodded.

"Think she knew what she was doing?" he asked.

"Guess so. She succeeded."

"Have something to do with Kennedy?"

"Nah, not really. But that didn't help none. Things must've looked pretty grim."

"Maybe she didn't know what she was doing."

"She knew. She bought me and Jackie new shoes."

"Huh?"

"Did other stuff, too. Like she even bought a turkey for Thanksgiving and stuffed it and shit."

DeCenz thought a while and then said, "Well it was kind of nice of her to buy a bird to get you guys through the funeral and all."

The next night we fought a freak snow-storm and drove to a pick-up joint called The Edge. I saw two girls I'd always thought I loved slobbering over a couple of old men. These guys had to be thirty-five years old, but there they were rubbing their three-piece suits up against sixteen-year-old nipples. It wasn't fucking fair.

When I mentioned it to Mousy, I was crushed to learn that

the two girls had been getting slammed by everyone in town. "They been laying everything except the Alaska Pipeline," he said.

Ten draughts and a couple of shots of Wild Turkey later I went home with a girl from the Lonsdale section of town named Bunny Cote. I'd met her playing pinball. She was watching over my shoulder, her perfume as subtle as ammonia, so I pushed up a game for her. Must've thanked me ten times before she'd finished her first ball. It was kind of sad, as if no one had ever blown a single dime on the girl. It wasn't that Bunny was ugly; she wasn't. Her makeup was crusted over her cheeks like calamine lotion and her eyes were roped in with a thick liner that drained an inky dew into the corners, giving her sort of a sad, clowny look, but beneath it all she was pretty. And she had a major-league body.

Bunny had been in the old man's radiator shop a few times so we had something to talk about. When we were getting into her Vega, she told me that she lived with her parents. I thought about going for it right there in the car, but the seats were too cold. Besides, I was wearing long underwear. We decided to go to my house. The old man rarely budged after crashing.

When we got there, I told Bunny to sit on the sofa and be quiet. I tiptoed to the old man's bedroom door. The light was out, and I faintly heard him snoring.

"So this is the Pop's place," she said when I rejoined her.

"Yeah," I said.

Bunny looked around, nodding her approval. "Hot shit, I always wondered what the inside of Pop's place looked like. *Not too shabby.* Not too shabby at all. Pop's got good taste."

"A regular interior decorator," I said.

"I love his sign on his shop," Bunny said, laughing as if she hadn't driven past it a thousand times in the past fifteen years. " 'A great place to take a leak.' That's so funny."

I groaned. "Yeah, yeah, yeah. Listen, you want something to eat?"

"Oh, no thanks. I had a sangwich before I went out tonight. Gotta watch my gut or it'll blow up on me. Ain't exactly no spring chicken, you know." She was eighteen.

"How about some soda or something?"

"Nope," she said, squeezing out a roll of flab on her thigh. "I'm starting to get that cellophone stuff around my ass."

"I have an idea," I said. "Hawaiian Punch. It's ten percent real fruit juice."

"That'd be terrific."

When I returned with her juice, Bunny was beating the shit out of my English bulldog, Patty. The old man had bought the dog when Jackie came home from the hospital. I think he got it off Caveech because English bulldogs cost an arm and a leg. The old man named the pup "Patriarca," after Raymond L.S. Patriarca, the head of the New England mob, a Providence resident, and the old man and Caveech's supposed *Goombah* (although, as far as I could tell, Raymond—as they chummily called him—didn't know they existed.)

Patty had been awakened by the sticking sound of the ice-box door opening and closing. Her droopy eyes were rimmed green with mucus and she looked pretty beat, but she knew it was a good bet I'd turn her on to a late-night snack. Instead, Dildo's date was knocking her all over the room. "Come on, you ugly boxer," Bunny said, leading with a left jab. "You look like you ran into a Mack truck. Come on, boxer"—Wham!—

"Come on, you old boxer"—Slap-a-dadap-dap!—"Come on, boxer"—Bang!—"Come on, yeah, come on"—Wap! She continued to batter Patty with a flurry of backhands.

"Hey, Bunny," I said, "I'd stop antagonizing that dog if I were you. She might snap at you."

Bunny dropped her dukes and gave me the once over. "Whoooaaa," she said. *"Antagonize,* the big words. Where'd you dig that one up, in the library or something?"

I put my hand on her leg, just above the knee.

"Guess the name of the state I'm thinking of," I said.

"What do you mean?" Bunny yelled.

"Shhh. Just try to guess the name of the state I'm thinking of."

"What the fuck, there's fifty-two friggin' states, Bimbo. How the hell am I—"

"Okay, okay, I'll give you a clue. It's an eastern state."

"Oh. California?"

"Wrong." I moved my fingers up a little. "That's West Coast, anyway. I'm thinking East Coast."

"Oh, ummm . . . Washington?"

"Nope." The hand went up another couple inches. "Bunny, we *live* on the East Coast."

She guessed a few midwestern states, and soon my hand was all the way up to her crotch. I started rubbing, and she kept on guessing.

"I know!" she said. "New England!"

"No, listen—"

"It's got be!" she yelled. "We live in New England."

"Keep it down. Forget it. It's a lousy game anyway."

"That was it, wasn't it? Come on, that was it, right?"

She was practically screaming.

"Yeah, shh, okay, okay, clam up. That was it. You win."

I was bummed out but determined to make the most of the situation. I turned off the lights. Bunny didn't object. Soon we were swapping spit. I was pleased with the situation; it had even stopped snowing. Then it happened. While my lips were working their way down her neck and my fingers were kneading her cow-like breasts, Bunny decided to drain her nasal passages. She snorted, grunted, growled, and ultimately coughed up a bronchial biscuit. There was an abrupt halt in the action as I wondered what she was going to do with the thing. Would she spit it outside? Spit it in the house? Or would she dare . . . ? In the meantime, Bunny cradled a multi-colored quag between the tip of her tongue and her lower lip.

Finally, she said, "Be wight back."

She went into the bathroom.

I sat on the sofa listening to the deep rumble of her throat.

"Hurry up!" I whispered frantically as she stepped out of the bathroom. "Out the front!" I grabbed her arm and, looking anxiously toward the old man's room, rushed her to the door.

"What's matter?" she asked.

"He's up!"

"Who?"

"The old man! You woke him up! He'll kill you!"

"Pop? He likes me."

"He's not rational at this hour. Run for it!"

Bunny hurried down the steps and struggled through the knee-deep snow. She didn't look back until she got to the Vega.

I waved her on.

My number-one priority in the spring

term was to make the baseball team. I hadn't played organized ball in a couple of years, but I knew I could pick it back up quickly. Unfortunately, I fanned my first nine times up and was cut from the team. The problem was that I'd played a lot of Whiffle ball the previous summer on Suicide, and I'd picked up some bad habits. You know, you start thinking you're King Kong. You can hitch, step in the bucket, roll your wrists all over town, and still pull the ball. Not in hardball. I'd be standing there waving the bat like Hank Aaron, and by the time I started swinging, the ball would already be in the catcher's mitt. First cut. Take a hike. I ended up playing for the J.V.s.

All spring, Jonathan Wheeler chased after S.D. Stuart. Because she was straight as an arrow, Wheeler came on like Steve Garvey. He agreed with her that no one should smoke or drink until they were at least in college (even though he got shit-faced three or four nights a week), and he never missed an opportunity to open a door or pull out a chair while pointing out my lack of manners. I was a derelict, he told her. You wouldn't believe Dunphy, he should be incarcerated, the craziest kid alive, and so forth.

Because Wheeler was too afraid to be alone with her, he always dragged me along. But the more I fucked off around S.D., the more she smiled. Then one day I received an ornate, cutesy-pie, amazingly folded note via one of S.D.'s friends inviting me up to the Girls School for a Saturday night Sadie Hawkins wingding. Wheeler was stunned. I felt sort of bad.

Even suggested that maybe I should blow it off. He told me to go, though, "just to see what she wants." We both figured it was a subtle ploy aimed at making him jealous.

S.D. and I went out during April and May. She was one of the two or three most popular girls in the school, and at first I was happy about her liking me but for some reason I couldn't maintain the feeling. S.D. Stuart had a four-year-old's nose, well-bred cheekbones, a sturdy if large toilet, and those naturally pouty lips earned from years of practice. She was extremely cool, rarely was impressed enough to laugh, wore a batch of wonderful-smelling perfumes and makeups, never let a hair fall out of place, and had nothing in common with me. What I called an alley, she called a cul-de-sac. I wanted to go out in the woods and drink beer, she'd just as soon sit in her room and read *The Bell Jar* for the seventeenth time. S.D. claimed to be "averse to premarital intimacy." (At this point, I was told, she was a virgin. "The furthest anyone ever got with her," Jonathan Wheeler said, "was when Les O'Neill stink-fingered her at a movie last fall." Wheeler knew this because he'd sniffed O'Neill's finger during intermission.)

Every few days we'd stroll into town for crescent rolls and Italian coffee and discuss fashion trends with a handful of S.D.'s small-nosed friends. The girls were constantly trying to outdo each other with tales of twenty-thousand-dollar expense accounts at Bloomie's, Saks, and so on.

Our dates would conclude with the two of us violently sucking each other's tongue moments before she boarded the bus back to the Girls School. It was as if the bus spewed some kind of magic exhaust. Every time that big, yellow monster came rumbling into sight S.D. would lean into me with a passionate, grinding embrace, I'd have just enough time to pop a woody and slide my hand over her bullet-proof bra, and then the bus would carry her and the other laughing girls away, roaring over my pathetic pup tent.

The two or three school dances we went to were exercises in humility. I stood in a corner with my knuckles up my ass while she took turns dancing with different guys. S.D. was "gunning" for one of the Top Ten positions appointed to juniors before their senior year. The school picked these leaders purely on the basis of how much of a kiss-ass, or "gunner," you were. Gunners were historically a prideless bunch, and S.D. Stuart proved that history repeats itself. She'd rat on her roommate to clinch an appointment to the Top Ten. So if her roommate wanted a smoke she had to hide from S.D. One day over the crescents and Italian Joe, she outlined her policy to me.

"You fink," I said. "How could you turn in your own roommate?"

"Oh, *shut up*. You make it sound like I'd be stabbing her in the back."

"You would be."

"Rubbish," S.D. said. "She knows perfectly well that her smoking puts me in a precarious position with the administration—and I've asked her several times to simply smoke elsewhere . . . or not at all."

"Excuse the expression, but I still think that's fucked up."

"Well that's too bad but I'm not going to compromise my beliefs just for her filthy habits. And by the way, *nice language.*" She served me one of her lemony squints.

"Come off it, S.D. Half the people in the world smoke butts, and nobody except the surgeon general says tiddly-poo about it. Besides, those aren't *your* beliefs. They're Cornwall Academy's beliefs, and you're just one of the tools they use to grind their fu—riggin' rules into everyone else's head."

S.D. didn't speak to me for a week. It was kind of nice having a seven-day hiatus from the runs (coffee opens me up like you wouldn't believe), but I regretted pissing her off. I think I missed having plans made for me. Every day Wheeler would ask me, "Any word from S.D.?" and "Hey, are you two still seeing each other, or what?" These questions were always accompanied by an ear-to-ear grin, but I guess I had that coming.

"Don't let it get you down," Irving said to me one night during study period. He'd been sitting at his desk reading the *Wall Street Journal.* I looked up from a *National Lampoon.* "Huh?"

"S.D. Don't let her get to you."

"I won't," I said. "She ain't my type anyway."

"I know what you're going through. Had the very same thing happen to me last summer. I was taking out this absolutely stunning gal, and after about three dates she told me to stop calling her."

I felt bad that Irving would confess this just to make me feel better.

"She give you any reason?" I asked.

"Not really. Just said she wanted to date more interesting guys."

"Oh."

He took a snapshot out of his wallet.

"Here's a picture of her."

It was apparently the girl's prom picture because she was wearing a gown, holding flowers, and standing in front of a maroon velvet curtain. It looked as if she didn't have a date, or, possibly, he was just embarrassed to stand beside her. One thing was for sure, she was one of the ugliest wenches I'd ever laid eyes on.

"Boy," I said, "she's quite a looker."

"Unfortunately, she knows it."

I nodded.

"She can get anybody she wants so what does she need me for?"

"Oh, come on," I said. "That's a pussy attitude. You can get any girl you want, too, Irv. You've just got to believe in yourself a little more."

"Oh yeah, sure. I can get any girl I want."

"That's right. You can get any *thing* you want for that matter. Because you're smarter than one hundred percent of the people in the world."

"Dunph . . . that's impossible. A hundred percent of the people would have to include me. How can I be smarter than myself?"

I thought about this. "See?"

I finally bumped into S.D. after one of my classes up at the Girls School. Tried to apologize but she said, "Drop it." She asked me to join her for lunch in the Girls Dining Hall.

We sat at a table that included a Top Ten member named Courtney Kingswood, two other seniors, two freshmen, and a junior named Jane Weston. I had heard locker room moanings about Jane Weston's beauty (for instance: "I'd swim a mile in shark-infested piss just to hear her fart over the phone.") but I'd never gotten a good close-up of her.

Jane was about five feet seven inches with shoulder-length, thick brown hair and amazing blue eyes. Her smile was warm and happy, and her skin had that golden glow that children get from playing outdoors in the winter. She had a strong voice—with a trace of a southern accent—which always sounded on the verge of a wonderful laugh. Her body was slender and athletic, and she had the nicest set of cupcake tits I'd ever seen. But the killer was those eyes; the bluest I'll ever see.

During the moments I managed to withdraw my attention from Jane, I couldn't believe the amount of shit that Courtney, S.D., and another one of the seniors were giving to one of the freshmen. Do this, don't do that, do this over again only do it right this time, and while you're there, pushead, get this and tell so and so something else. On the double! I asked S.D. why they were giving the little kid so much grief, and she said it was because the girl had an "attitude." Meaning she wasn't kissing anyone's ass.

The moment the freshman returned with dessert she was ordered back to the kitchen for seconds.

"I'll get it," I said. "Have something to eat."

"No, you *won't* get *anything*," said Courtney. "I addressed *her* and like don't interfere. Besides, guys aren't allowed in the kitchen."

"Then I'll go in drag," I said, smiling, as I stood up.

"Sit down!" Courtney screamed. "Now!"

I stopped smiling. "Then send someone else," I said. I held the girl's hand and kept her from returning to the kitchen.

"Don't tell me who to send, buster. *I'm* the head of this table, so you just shut up and eat."

Suddenly Jane Weston darted from the table. She was in the kitchen before anyone could stop her. Courtney was fuming. S.D. was shooting me daggers. When Jane returned, Courtney stood and said, "Weston, don't ever again *dare* pull that crap with me. I-tell-who-does-what. Okay? You got it?"

"Sorry, Sarge," Jane said.

Three minutes hadn't passed and Courtney was telling the freshman to clear the table. When the girl tried to wolf down one last forkful of chow, Courtney grabbed her wrist and said, "Now!"

I slammed my hand on the table and said, "Leave her alone, you twat!" Maybe not the best choice of words. You could've heard an ant fart.

"That's five hours," Courtney said, "and you can shove off now, buster."

S.D. was glaring at me as if I'd cut her Bloomie's card in half.

I felt nervous. The girls' ears at the surrounding tables seemed to focus in my direction. The freshman was frantically clearing the table when I stood up. I put my plate on the tray for her. "Good luck," I said.

At this, Courtney let out an absolutely witchy cry, banged her fists on the table, and shrieked, "Get out!"

I was more than happy to. For a second I'd had this awful vision of being forced to duke it out with Courtney, the two of us rolling in the aisle amidst a ring of chanting women. As I was leaving, Jane Weston said, "Bye."

That evening someone handed me a typed letter from S.D. It was only folded in half. Calling me, believe it or not, a "boorish churl," she asked that I "henceforth desist from acknowledging" her. Everything was precise and orderly. Like a form letter. By the weekend she would be going steady with Jonathan Wheeler.

The next day Courtney stung me eight hours: three for "insubordination" and five for "profanity." Worse, she had every bounty-hunter Top Ten member on my case. Failing to button my top button at breakfast, playing pocket pool with myself during chapel—they'd sting me for anything. A senior named Grant Bowzer even stung me an hour for walking past an M&M's wrapper that was tumbleweeding across one of the paths that dissect the campus.

I went to my Norman Vincent Peale-ish advisor, Mr. Cole, for advice. Definitely the wrong guy to lean on. Cole was tall and skinny, had an Adam's apple the size of a three-wood, and was a born-again marshmallow. With Cole it was never sudden death, it was sudden *victory*. His glass was always half *full,* and he was thirty-seven years *young*. On the day I saw him it was partly *sunny* out. (I heard later that Cole had twice tried to do himself in.) Naturally, his advice was to "just forget it."

"What do you mean, 'forget it'?" I asked as he expertly led me to the door.

"Don't worry about a thing, big fella, you're going to be all right."

"Well, thanks," I said, and he closed the door in my face with a satisfied smile.

Just when I'd come to accept my fate, one of the outfielders on the baseball team got thrown out of school, and, since I'd

been doing pretty well on the J.V. team (when I wasn't working hours), I got brought up to the big club. I hated the chick-
enshit hypocrisy of riding the pines for the varsity when I
could've been playing regularly for the J.V.'s, but somehow this
earned me respect and the Grant Bowzers of the world started
thinking twice before stinging me. Which is human nature.

The next weeks passed uneventfully, and

before I knew it I was taking my final exams. Didn't do very
well on them, pulling a C/D average. I couldn't complain; it
would've been a solid D if not for my physics teacher cutting
me some slack.

The teacher, a fossil named Mr. Howell, had told us the
day before the exam that anyone who didn't bring his own slide
rule would get an automatic F. He didn't want anyone passing
rulers covered with answers, and the test promised to be a
bitch. I stayed up all night cramming and remembered to bring
a slide rule. Unfortunately, Wheeler, sitting behind me, forgot
his, and since the ruler only came into play on a third of the test
and he was giving me a headache, I let him borrow mine at the
beginning of class. I breezed through two-thirds of the exam
and then waited for my ruler. And waited. Finally, I whispered
over my shoulder, "Hey, Wheeler, give the ruler back." He
didn't look up.

When there were about twenty minutes to go, I said,
"Come on, cough it up."

Wheeler leaned forward. "Stop worrying, moron. I'll write
the answers on the back."

"Don't do me any favors. Just give me the ruler."

With about two minutes left, he slid the ruler up the aisle. Ten feet past my seat. Just as I was about to make a dash for it, the kid whose seat it was laying beside picked it up and began checking the answers with his own. I considered walking over and ripping it out of his slimy hands, but I noticed a teacher named Mr. Swanson watching me. Next thing I knew, Howell was collecting the tests and Jonathan Wheeler was reminding me that man decides his own fate and I didn't have to give him the ruler in the first place.

"You killed me," I said.

"Spare me the heartache," Wheeler said, "I never held a gun to your head."

I went back to my room and crashed. Woke up at six o'clock, depressed. I sat on the edge of my bed, not having enough energy to pull the shades or reach for the light. A soft knock sounded on the door. Wheeler, I figured. "Go away," I groaned. The door, however, opened, and in the doorway appeared an adult figure. I couldn't make out who it was but he could see me all right, sitting there in the dark, eyes puffed, sporting a chaotic mound of bedhead.

Mr. Swanson asked if he could turn on the light.

"Sure," I said.

He came in and leaned against my desk. I didn't move, just sat there in my boxer shorts.

"I'd like to have a chat with you."

"About what?"

"About today. I saw what went on during the test."

"Yeah . . . ?"

"You were cheating."

"Well, no—"

"When you gave Wheeler your slide rule, that was cheating."

I sighed.

"Look, Mr. Swanson—"

"Dave."

He was a young guy, just out of Amherst College, which turned out to be a lucky break.

"Um . . . I didn't mean to cheat, I was just—"

"Trying to pass?"

"Well yeah, I mean no. I knew it . . . for the most part. I needed the ruler. It was mine, you know."

"I told Mr. Howell you got ill. So he passed you."

I didn't get it.

"Jonathan Wheeler is poison, Dunph. Stay away from him. And have a nice summer."

PART *Three*

I spent the summer of '74 in hazy Falmouth, Massachusetts, a resort town on Cape Cod. The old man finagled me a job at a caddy camp, and the day I returned from school he dropped me off on Route 195 with a cardboard sign that read: Cape Cod or Vicinity.

I passed the time on the sweltering golf course daydreaming about Jane Weston. I would've given anything to have known her well enough to get in touch with her. I felt as if I *did* know her, but the fact was that I didn't really, and I was resigned to daydream. "Daydreaming" is an understatement; during that summer I must have logged a thousand hours thinking about the girl.

I left the Cape on August 30 and returned to Pawtucket for the remaining two weeks of vacation. On my first night back the old man sat me down for a discussion.

"So you had a big time this summer, eh Dildo?"

"Yeah, pretty good time."

"Well, don't you think it's about time you started producing? You know, you *are* getting a little old for that garbage."

"What garbage? You were the one who sent me out to the Cape."

"To work. Not to stay out until four every night chasing

pussy and acting like a wise guy. I pull a few strings, get you into a nice school, and now you think you're a big spender who can chase pussy and act like a wiseguy. Drinks are on Dildo. Everyone's buddy, right? WRONG!"

"But—"

"And don't give me any lip. You'll wish you never learned to talk."

I listened.

"You know that school you go to? You see any of your spinach-chin friends going there? No. Why do you think that is? Why do you think that is you're the only punk in Pawtucket that goes to a fucking prep school? Because of connections! Caveech got more pull in that place than Raymond got in his little finger. But you don't appreciate it. And I get you a job on the Cape Cod—*madonne,* what I wouldn't give for a job on the Cape Cod when I was a kid—but, no, you don't appreciate it. You don't appreciate nothing."

"Okay, I appreciate it. Why can't I enjoy myself, too. I saved five hundred bills—"

"Four-fifty," the old man said. "I got fifty coming off the top."

"For what?"

"I lent you fifty frogpelts when you went to your school last year."

"Thirty! I *asked* for fifty."

"You owe me fifty, Dildo, and don't make me start adding it up because you wouldn't have a pot to piss in if it wasn't for me. I don't know too many kids that get brand new drums for their birthday. My old man never bought that for *me.*"

"Pop, come on, they were bongos, and that was eight years ago."

"So what? I didn't charge you nothing then, did I? You know what those things would be worth today?"

"Listen," I said, "didn't you ever have no fun when you were my age?"

"Ah fongoo. Don't tell me what I was doing at your age, buddy. When I was your age, I was working seven days a week from sunup to sundown at the Old Brown Millinery trying to earn enough frogpelts so that I could afford the privilege of going to a trade school. That's right, *privilege.*"

When he continued with this line of bullshit, I couldn't help but tune out. I wondered if in the year 2000 I would be giving my kid this kind of lecture. Would I brag about saving my pennies to buy a nickel of weed and frugally scraping my bongs to smoke the resin? Would I call him a spoiled brat for throwing away roaches?

Finally, I said, "Well good, you went, didn't you?"

The old man paused, baffled. "Went where?"

"To trade school. You should be happy; you got what you wanted."

The old man's nostrils shivered. He gave me his Jackie-Gleason-pissed-off look. To the moon, Dildo! "You know," he said, "sometimes you're about as sharp as a bowling ball. All you think about is having a good time. Well, the good times is over, Dildo. It's time you stopped being an underachiever and start working to your potential." He spread his arms, and his lips puckered up like a tuba. "PRODUCE!!!"

I leaned back.

"You're going to have to get your grades way up this year," the old man said, "because if you want to live a comfortable life, you're going to have to get into a good college and then get a good job where you can make *good* money. Capisce?"

"That all that matters to you? Money? What, you think you've got to have money to be happy?"

"Absolutely! If you don't remember no other advice I ever gave you, remember this, Dildo . . ." Suddenly, tires screeched out at the intersection. The old man jerked his head to the window but there was no crack-up. He lowered his voice and leaned toward me. "Life," he said, "is like a shit sandwich: The more bread you got, the less shit you eat."

In a burst of boldness, I said, "Then let me ask you this: Why is it that it's the big rich execs who are always diving off the fourteenth floor head first?"

"Don't be a *Portagee,*" he said. "Those are the guys that just lost all their bread, dummy."

That's the way the old man was. Had decent intentions, I guess, but he always expressed them in a fucked-up way. I remember coming home from fifth grade with a so-so report card and the not-so-old man slapping me in the head and saying, "Okay, keep it up, Dildo. Next they'll be sending *you* over to get killed in Vietnam. That's right, kid. First they draft all the fucknuts who flunk out of school, and then they take the douchebags who bring home report cards like this. You want to get your head blowed off? Good, then keep it up. You're well on your way."

Before letting me out after the Shit Sandwich sermon, the old man informed me that my scholarship had been trimmed in accordance with the school's recent cutbacks and, instead of my previous $500, I was going to have to cough up a grand. Attached to the form that outlined my payment plan was a letter pleading for more contributions to the Cornwall Academy Annual Fund.

Old C.A. was clearly wallowing in some rough financial straits. They were soliciting any kind of offering: memorial gifts, charitable gifts, trusts, stocks, property, anything. The school was even inaugurating a new program called the Cornwall Academy Friends of Austerity Fund. Morgan Brewster, the Annual Fund's chairperson and author of the solicitation, was obviously shitting his pants. Several times in the letter he referred to a "threatening state of insolvency." His closing sentence was, "The Academy can still have a prosperous and exciting future but your support is needed *NOW!*"

"Listen," the old man said as I was leaving the house, "you only got to pay me thirty bucks but I do want that."

"Thanks," I said. "I appreciate it. Can I keep the bongos, too?"

"Get outta here, smart guy."

At the Hilltop Cafe Mousy was sitting alone in a booth by the door. It was the first time I'd seen the guys since they'd driven down the Cape for Fourth of July weekend.

Mousy looked startled to see me. He seemed haggard, different.

"Would've been up here earlier but the load has been on my case," I said.

"Huh."

He stared out the window, silent. I tried to recall if I'd said anything over Fourth of July to piss him off. DeCenz and Tommy the Wire brought over a pitcher of 'Gansett and slid into the booth.

"You hear the news?" DeCenz said.

"No, what?"

I took a sip from Tommy's glass.

"The Wire here is in love."

"Oh, fuck you," the Wire said, "I ain't in love with no-body."

"You sure?" DeCenz asked. "That's not what she thinks."

I couldn't believe how different Mousy acted. He was slumped in his seat. Something out in the oil-stained parking lot had his attention.

"Good," the Wire said. "She can think whatever she wants to think as long as she keeps that little flapper available."

"Wire," I said, "you got a new mule?"

"Yeah. A real bimbo."

"Who?"

"Debbie Sylvia."

"She any good?"

"Not bad. On a scale of one to ten I'd put her about one bra size shy of a nine."

I waited for Mousy to set him straight with his advice that "tits are for kids," but he didn't.

"You should see this chick's nipples," the Wire said. "Exactly where they should be."

"Right on the end of her tits?" I said, taking another sip of beer.

"You know what I mean," he said. "Up high, real firm."

"How long you been seeing her?"

"About two weeks but I did her about a month before that."

DeCenz laughed.

"I dragged her out of January's one night and hosed her right out in the parking lot," the Wire said. "Then I'm in there a couple of weeks ago and this fucking incredible babe comes up to me and goes, 'You almost gave me whiplash, buddy,' and I looked at her like I never seen her before, I was so cocked when I did her, so I asked her out."

"That's fucking precious," I said.

"Yeah. The thing what's fucked up is I didn't even remember her name and she loved my ass."

"This babe tight?" DeCenz asked.

"Fuck, yeah," the Wire said. "I'm talking shoehorn city."

DeCenz smiled. "Tell him how often you bang her."

"A lot," the Wire said. "And I mean we do everything: 69, 42, 37, hershey highway, you name it. You know, I asked her to enter into a relationship. I told her, 'None of this once-a-week-or-no-blow-job shit.' I go, 'I want a girl who's gonna swallow my dick, balls, and asshole at the same time.' "

"Beautiful," I said. "All three at once."

Tommy the Wire nodded.

"Show Dunph what she gave you on your tongue," DeCenz said, and my heart sank.

The Wire showed DeCenz his middle finger.

"Come on," DeCenz said.

"Fuck off. I told you before it's just a canker, and, anyway, I didn't get it from Debbie. I got it from that Cranston chick."

"A canker, huh. Dunph, do you get cankers that last for three weeks?"

"Wire," I said, "why'd you let me drink out of your glass if your mouth is fucked up?"

" 'Cause booze kills things. And anyway, it ain't catchy. If it was, then Debbie'd have it all over her ass."

I wiped my tongue with a napkin.

"Go ahead," DeCenz said, "show him it, pimplebreath. This is the '70s, everyone gets social diseases."

"What is it you got?" I asked.

"Asshole thinks I got the drip because I hosed some bushpig from Cranston and my tongue got fucked up."

"How fucked up?"

"Not really fucked up. Just, you know, a little. Like it feels sort of burnt. Probably just a canker."

"You do any diving?" DeCenz asked.

"On who?"

"The pig."

"No fucking way!"

"How does your pecker feel?" I asked.

"Actually, it feels a little funny when I piss."

"What do you mean 'funny'?"

"Well, you know, sort of like I'm pissing razor blades. Look, I ain't going to no doctor until I absolutely gotta. Last time I got my worm checked the Doc stuck a Q-Tip up there like he was loading a fucking cannon. Felt like I got electrocuted."

For the next few hours, the Wire and DeCenz filled me in on what had been happening on Suicide. Mousy just stared out at the Hilltop parking lot and smoked butts. The few times he did speak it was in a strained and somehow embarrassing voice. Everyone felt uneasy. At the end of the night a sullen, almost robotic Mousy dropped DeCenz and me off at a Del's Lemonade stand a few blocks from my street. We walked the rest of the way sipping frozen lemonade which we'd mixed with vodka.

"What's with Mousy these days?" I asked. "He's acting like he's on drugs or something."

"Yeah, he's on drugs all right. He's doing greens."

"Greens?"

"He's been on a big *money* kick. Talking about moving down to Jersey and working for some nuclear power plant."

"Come on?!"

"I'm serious."

"What about 'Zona?"

DeCenz clicked his tongue. "Christ, Arizona's been out of the picture since June. Ain't enough money in 'Zona. He's thinking of either Connecticut or Jersey."

"I don't believe it," I said.

"I'll wipe both your asses for a week if I'm wrong."

We finished the spiked slush on my front steps. After a while DeCenz stopped being a hard-ass. He was just concerned for Mousy, not pissed off at him. "Don't know what's gotten into him, Dunph, but all of a sudden the kid's talking about selling out. You know, a house in the city, two point three kids, a nine-to-five job, your basic Mr. Nobody trip."

"Nuclear power plants?" I said. *"New Jersey?!* If only he could hear himself, he'd shit his pants."

"Yeah, and if your aunt had balls, she'd be your uncle. I'm telling you, he's been listening to his money-hungry uncles, and

he's fucking brainwashed. It's hopeless, man." DeCenz hesi-
tated and then said, "Somebody should pull the plug on the
guy."

The day I thumbed back to Cornwall was beautiful and
depressing. Overnight it had become sweater-and-football
weather. The sky was bluer and the world clearer. It *looked*
September.

The next morning my advisor, Mr. Cole, entered my room,
steady as a house of cards. When the weakling failed to hint
what was troubling him, I asked, "Wasn't I invited back this
year?"

Cole closed his eyes and raised a hand. "No, no, Timothy. I
mean yes, yes, you're all right."

"Who died then?" I asked with a nervous smile.

"Well, I . . . uh. . . ." his voice faded.

"Mr. Cole, what's the matter?"

"Well, uh, Dean Mort asked that I speak to you."

"Then speak, speak."

"Speak," he repeated, and that big, ripe Adam's apple
bobbed around out of control.

I started feeling very afraid.

"I told the Dean I'm not good at this," he said. "I told
him."

There was another pause, and then Cole broke from the
room, saying, "Call home, Timothy!"

I'm not usually a gory bastard but I think I owned the record for looking at Mousy at the wake. When my turn came to kneel in front of his open coffin, I couldn't get back up. One by one at least twenty twitching mourners knelt beside me, prayed, and scurried away. It's not that I'm a sucker for long goodbyes. For most of the trance I wasn't even looking at Mousy; I just stared at the silky purple lining on the inside of the casket, confused by his family's morbid ambition. They'd shaved off his beard and given him a crew cut.

"Your buddy looked pretty good with a pineapple," the old man said after the wake. He was watching a *Gilligan's Island* rerun. "Hardly recognized him."

"That's because you never saw him dead before."

"Nah, it was the hair. He should've chopped that fucking mop off a long time ago."

"You're unbelievable," I said.

He finally looked up. "What, you're pissed at me because the poor asshole gets crocked and runs into a pole at five in the morning?"

"Three in the morning," I yelled, "and what the fuck does it matter what time it was?! He didn't deserve to die!"

"Come here," he said.

I didn't budge.

"I said come here."

I moved next to his chair.

"You looking for a shot?"

I nodded no.

He gave me a shot across the side of the head. He had to reach up though and didn't really connect.

"You looking for a shot?" he asked again.

"No," I said.

"Say it then. You answer me when I talk to you."

"No, I don't want a shot, okay?"

"Don't give me that shit, Dildo. I didn't kill your friend."

It was ironic, though, that Mousy should be the one to fulfill the old man's fantasy. Right in front of our house. The Big One. The accident, I figured from the fragments of hearsay I collected at the wake and S.R.O. funeral, was a "momentarily lost control and slammed into a telephone pole" type of bang-up. Adults speculated in their cars about drugs and booze. When the oinkers arrived at the scene, Mousy was already dead. They said he never felt a thing. He'd hit the pole so hard that the tire had flown off the car. Bunny Cote was with him, which surprised me more than anything. She was in shock (although hardly hurt at all) and had been unable to give any further details.

The night after Mousy was buried, DeCenz and I stood in front of the bruised wooden pole. Lighting the sprinkled windshield into worthless diamonds was one of those streetlights that you only find in cities or near Cumberland Farms stores, a brutally bright, almost fluorescent, white light with a blue halo around it. We smoked a bone and stared at the diamonds.

"Hey, Dunph, when someone says they slept like a baby, does that mean they slept good or bad?"

"Good."

"That's what I thought, but it don't make no sense. I mean babies shit their pants and end up crying at four in the morning."

I thought about this. "I guess they're talking about how babies get rocked to sleep by their mothers and how they don't really have a worry in the world."

"I see what you mean."

This seemed to remind DeCenz where we were.

"Fuck," he said. *"Fuck."*

For over an hour we threw rocks at the streetlight, trying to break its gruesome glare. It was useless; the cover must've been made of some kind of unbreakable plastic. I considered using the old man's .45, but I didn't want to touch it. Then the clouds that had hung low and pregnant throughout the day burst, and the two of us ran from the streetlight toward our fading shadows to the Dunphy front porch.

PART *Four*

Back at school I tried to forget. Which was impossible. I couldn't read more than a paragraph before my mind would drift and I'd catch myself smiling about something Mousy had said. I'd remember that the good feeling was only in my mind and get depressed. I sighed a lot. Usually I'd bag the books and end up bullshitting the night away with the guys on my hall.

Jonathan Wheeler didn't soothe my spirit any. "Dunphy, I understand that a friend of yours bit the dust," he said after barging into my room. His roommate, Candle (dubbed because of an ear condition that often left golden rivers of wax clotted over his earlobes), stood behind him peeling the rind off an orange that was smudged with fingerprints, like an old baseball.

"Yeah," I said warily.

"Well, you'd better just forget about it because there's not a damn thing you can do. He's history."

"God must have something better planned for him," Waltham added.

Wheeler looked at Waltham and smiled. "God?" he said. "Don't tell me that you morons still believe in *God?*"

Waltham and I looked at each other and nodded. I always believed in God when I was scared shitless. But in my heart I was a C and E Catholic and wasn't entirely sold on the God thing. The two times I went to church each year (Christmas and Easter) weren't enough to rope me in.

"Sorry, kiddies," Wheeler said. "I hate to burst your biblical bubbles, but he does *not* exist. Uh-uh, no way. Pure theological bufferoonery." Counting on his fingers, he said, "Santa Claus, the Easter Bunny . . . *God.*"

"Th-th-that's a bad thing to say," Waltham cried, "and it's a lie."

"A bad thing to say about whom? Santa Claus or the Easter Bunny?"

"You know who I mean."

"Oh, spare me the pious drivel, Waltham. God is an invention to keep morons like you from killing each other. Those who know that rule the world."

The fact that this guy would be living on my hall for a whole year drained me of energy. By June I would be up for sainthood or murder. Waltham and Wheeler volleyed back and forth reasons why there had to be and couldn't be a God. Wheeler was the better volleyer and kept jamming it down Irving's throat. I didn't say anything, just lay on my bed and prayed to God that I was praying to God—for Mousy's sake.

One clear morning toward the end of September, I slept through breakfast, showered, and decided for the first time in my life to blow dry my hair. You know how sometimes you wake up and you're just flat-out butt-ugly? Well I was nasty that morning. Big nose, puffy cheeks, swollen eyes, and a couple zits on my forehead that were quickly developing into antlers. So I decided to go with the ninety-mile-an-hour look to see if it would help any.

As I was walking to class I noticed something promising coming toward me on the boardwalk. My heart started thumping like a football in a clothes dryer. Jane Weston. As we converged, I glanced over and said, "What's uk?"

"Hi, Dunph," she said. "How're you doing?"

We stopped but continued leaning in the directions we were headed.

"Great. I'm fine." My voice sounded different, too articulate.

"Haven't seen you around at all this year," she said.

"Haven't seen you around at all this year," I repeated. I felt out of breath, and the corner of my eye began to twitch.

"Almost didn't recognize you," she said. "I remembered you as having much curlier hair."

I reached my hand to my head and blurted out, "Oh, I do, but I blow dried this morning." Then, "Uh, I don't usually, I never do, but this morning I was fooling around and, you know, I just, you know, I don't know." My antlers began to glisten as I confirmed that the blur I'd just seen was a gob of my spit aimed at her face. She wiped it off but kept smiling.

"See you around," she said and moved along.

"Did you have a nice summer?" I called, but she just walked away.

The next week I spotted Jane several times and it was becoming clear that she had the hots for a new kid named Jack Rafferty. Rafferty was a P.G. student—he'd come to Cornwall after graduating from his regular high school—and had quickly become the star quarterback. He also had black Irish Kennedy looks, a quick wit, and a gift for being extremely obnoxious without being too offensive. He and Jane always seemed to be having a great time, laughing or rushing around in the midst of some exciting plans.

At one of the daily assemblies during the second week of school, Dean Mort ordered Rafferty to stand and recite the Cornwall Academy Fight Song. Jack made up words to the tune of The Star Spangled Banner. He got so wrapped up in his performance that he began motioning for everyone to march around the room with him. Nobody did, of course, but it broke everyone up.

He walked into the dining hall for dinner that evening and got a standing ovation. Rafferty was in vogue, and I felt like a Nehru shirt. So I did what I always did when faced with stiff competition. I bought pot and got creative.

The next afternoon when I spotted Jane in the hall between classes, I walked up from behind and tapped her on the shoulder. She looked a little startled but said hi.

"Howdy," I said. "I, uh, noticed you checking me out over there."

She blinked. "You what?"

"I noticed you checking me out."

"What are you talking about?"

"Come on, let's cut the games, Jane. Every time I walk out of class you're hanging around here."

"That's right," she said in exasperation, "because I happen to be getting out of the class across the hall."

"Right, right. And I suppose you haven't been following me around all year. What, you think I'm stupid?"

"Yeah, I do. And I also think you're out of your frapping mind."

She walked away and I followed.

"Hey, I'm kidding," I said.

She stopped and glared at me.

"It was a joke," I said. "Ha ha. You know, just . . . a . . . joke."

"You're a real funny guy," she said dryly.

"Listen," I said, "do you by any chance like to get high?"

We spent that period and almost every free period for the next two weeks sitting up on the mountain beside Thames Brook talking and smoking bones. I was in heaven. At first I behaved sort of dumb about being alone with her in the woods—I dusted off a boulder for her to sit on once—but the more we talked, the looser I got, and the better we got along.

Because we came from different backgrounds—Jane was from Toms Brook, Virginia—we had a lot to gab about. I'd never seen a herd of deer in my backyard and she'd never seen a pack of rats in hers. Jane had a good sense of humor so I told her all my Dirty Ernie jokes and she didn't get offended. Also, I told her about my plans to move to Arizona and she seemed excited.

One day as I walked into the dining room for lunch, Jane waved me over to Rafferty's table. It was against school rules to sit in an unassigned seat but I took it as a challenge and accepted.

For most of lunch I kept my trap shut. Then Olga started jabbering about the crumbling love affair of Jonathan Wheeler and S.D. Stuart. "Jonathan broke up with S.D. over Columbus Day weekend," she announced.

"What a silly thing to break up over," I said.

"It's not funny, she's heartbroken. Should see her. She cried for three days and couldn't sleep a wink, so somebody gave her a bunch of Valiums and now she's walking around like a zombie. She's so depressed."

"I guess it's true then," Rafferty said. "Depression is the better part of Valium."

"You're a real punster," Jane said.

"What's two-thirds of a pun?" I asked.

"What?"

"P.U."

"S.D. is so in love," Olga cooed.

"Good God, Ogre, don't make us puke," Jack said. "You don't know what love is."

"Oh, and *you* do?"

"That's right," Jack said. "Love is being able to tell your girlfriend she has a snot on her nose. S.D.'s just horny and insecure. It's called withdrawal. She was getting the guy's pork, and now she doesn't know what she's gonna do."

"You've got some nerve," Olga said. "For your information, *they* had a platonic relationship."

"Yeah, right," Jack said. "They'd fuck their brains out and then talk about Plato. Just listen to yourself. She's walking around like a bowl of Maypo, right? She's insecure."

Olga forced an incredibly smug smile and said, "Jack, it's not *always* quiet people who are insecure. Usually it's the loud ones like you who are trying to hide something. It's a fact that class clowns are generally insecure, did you know that?"

"For your four-one-one, Ogre, yes, I did. And I'm secure

enough not to worry about generalizations. Now eat your fish, it's brain-food."

"How's S.D. now?" Jane asked.

"Terrible," Olga said. "She keeps skipping classes and she's getting stung all over the place. She just sits in the lounge all day watching television."

Dean Mort rang the dinner bell and stunned everyone by announcing that if the football team emerged victorious in the Big Game against Groate-Eldridge the next day, all of Monday's classes would be cancelled. The dining hall erupted for a full two minutes and then, as was traditional before the Big Game, eight or nine kids huddled in the middle of the room and screamed out the school fight song.

Afterward, Mort said that in his thirty years at Cornwall he couldn't recall himself or any of his predecessors ever announcing a holiday with a victory stipulation. "I don't know," he announced giddily, "perhaps I've gone crazy in my old age." In the awkward silence that followed, Jack Rafferty yelled out, "Oh, you thilly gooth!"

The entire dining hall laughed at Mort. I had to give Rafferty credit, it was a great crack. Some of the teachers even broke into smiles. Mort didn't, though. He got ruffled and embarrassed, but he never smiled. Neither did Rafferty.

Cornwall lost to Groate-Eldridge, 18–12, in

a mud bowl fought in forty-degree temperature during a vicious downpour. I stood there through the whole thing and awoke the following morning with a vise on my tonsils. It quickly loosened up, and the next couple nights I kept Waltham awake with my constant hacking and gurgling. On Tuesday I checked into the infirmary, the only building on campus that received heat twenty-four hours a day.

"That was some snooze, D-man," were the cheerful first words that I heard the next morning. Someone was resting on one elbow in the next bed. Layers of film slipped off my eyeballs.

"Rafferty," I said, "s'up?"

"Not much. Jesus, Mary, and Joseph, D-man, if you're gonna be crashing here again tonight, you're gonna have to do something about that lumberjacking. Good God, you've been sawing wood all morning."

Didn't have the energy to respond.

"I've been listening to you since 6:15," Rafferty said.

"Regular milkman."

"Yeah, I couldn't sleep because I was choking on snot so I dragged myself down here to drain."

"I can dig it," I said, and rolled over on my side, facing away from Rafferty.

For the next hour Rafferty went on about how much he hated the school and how he wished he were back home with the South Portland Red Riots.

"You must know what I mean, D-man," he said. "You don't seem like one of those hell-bent, gung-ho Corny assholes."

"Haven't exactly got a woody over the place."

"What do you think of Mort?"

I shrugged.

"Asshole of the year," he said. "He thinks he's the cat's nads."

"Uh-huh."

"You know what the dick does?"

"Uh-uh."

"He comes barging into my room the other night—by the way, these doors without locks," he lifted his hands, "what the hell, D-man. You can't even snap your beef in private. Anyway, this lunatic Mort comes barging into my room and he starts screaming at me like I've been caught probing his wife with a salami. I'm sitting there picking toejam and minding my own beeswax, and he stings me three hours. Says he doesn't like my act, that's all. You know why he's pissed? Do you know? I do. Because I arrived at Cornwall with a beard. You should've seen the looks. Might as well have been laying down lines at B.Y.U."

The nurse rushed into the room, took our temps, bitched about how unruly we were being, and told us to shut up. When she left, we looked at each other in bewilderment. I knew that under different circumstances I probably would have liked him.

"Your old man make you come here?" I asked.

"Good God, yeah. What do you take me for? You think I'd be here if I had any choice in the matter? Harvey all but forced me at gunpoint out of South Portland. It was either Cornwall or military school. He thinks this'll get me into an Ivy League school."

"It might."

"Fuck that. I told him I'm not going to even apply to any Ivies because I'd have to fellate too many people to get in."

"Harvey your old man?"

"Yeah. He couldn't handle the fact that I was a normal kid."

"What do you mean?"

"You know, D-man, he caught me shit-faced a few times, I cracked up his Mercedes, and I clinched a trip when one of his clients caught me siphoning gas out of his car."

That night, after noting that I'd been "quite the anti-social bastard," Jack said, "What's your prob?"

"Nothing. Just that I got this habit of not talking much when I feel like I'm gonna die. It's a Rhode Island thing."

"Come on," he said, "stop muffling your farts, man. Let's get it out in the open."

"Give me a break."

"Listen, D-man, I know that you've got a big dink for Weston, and you probably hate me because you think we've got something going on the side. Am I right?"

I didn't know what to say.

"You're barking up the wrong tree. I'm not interested in your chicken. If you knew me at all you'd know I'm a funbag man from way back. I adhere to the 3B principle: The Bigger the Boobs the Better. To tell you the truth, I'd really like to deal on Weston's friend, Cindy."

"Cindy?" I said. "You mean, Cindy with the—" I cupped my hands in front of my chest.

"Yeah, Cindy Biddle. The one who looks like the mouse-keteer, what's her name, Annette Funni-big-boobs."

"I always liked her, too," I lied.

"Amazing funbags, huh?"

"Majestic," I said.

"Unfortunately, she's going out with my roommate."

"You live with Creature?"

He nodded. "Dumbest motherfucker who ever lived."

I checked out of the infirmary the following morning and spent the next couple days dallying around Jane's friends, classrooms, and hangouts trying to enter her orbit. There was a dance coming up on Saturday night, but when Saturday rolled around and I still hadn't seen Jane, I took Jack up on an offer to party with him and his friends.

When I got to Rafferty's room at seven that night, I found Creature staring into a mirror examining his large, rubbery beer belly and bristly chest. His hair was wet, revealing a prematurely emerging scalp. A damp bar of soap camouflaged with pubes rested in a puddle on the dresser beside him. Standing with just a towel around his waist, he was idly singing "You'll Never Get to Heaven if You Break My Heart." Except Creature sang, "You'll never get to heaven if you smell my farts." He was probably right.

"Excuse me," I said, "is Jack around?"

He continued his serenade.

I tapped on the door and said, "Yo, I was supposed to meet Jack up here around seven."

Creature faced me and snorted. "Yo, he'll be right back." With his Flintstone's beard and puffy face, he didn't look a day under thirty-five.

He walked over, looked me in the eye, belched heartily, and then asked, "Get any on you?"

"No, I don't think so," I said.

"You lucked out."

A sour expression twisted Creature's lips, and, having grabbed a comb off his closet shelf, he stomped back to the mirror.

Jack walked in the room. "D-man, you fuckhead, you made it!"

I smiled.

"Sorry I'm late, man, but I have some serious bitch troubles. You meet Creech?"

"Yeah," I said. "He's been super."

Jack handed me a six-pack of St. Pauli Girl beer.

"What's this stuff?" I said. "Never heard of it."

"Me neither," said Jack, "but it was the beer nearest to the door so I grabbed a case and bolted."

Creature pulled on a dungaree jacket for a shirt and headed out.

"Can you believe that fucker?" Jack said. "He's scary, man."

I flipped open a bottle on the corner of a desk.

"I didn't know you had a babe to have trouble with," I said.

"I don't really. Just this slut I grabbed at the beginning of the year. Had to set her straight. It's weird, Dunph. Just because you stick your dick in them, they think it means something."

"You guys drink up here much?" I asked.

"Never."

"Want to take off?"

"Yeah."

I moved toward the door. He opened the window.

"Out this way," he said.

"On the *gutter?*" We were on the fourth floor.

"Sure. Drinks are on the house. That way the beer stays cold, no one can see you, and you couldn't ask for a better view of the moon reflecting off the sludge in the Hoozy. It's the cat's nads."

"I bet," I said.

Getting out onto the ledge was no problem, and, because it was too dark to see how high up I was, I didn't get too freaked out. However, I was a tad wary of the rusty two-foot-wide gutter that our lives were tottering on. After a couple beers, I relaxed enough to start enjoying the scenery. Another beer and I was becoming quite the daredevil, venturing a few feet to either side of the window. After four or five pops we began harmonizing on "Up on the Roof," and by the time we'd each finished a six-pack, I was dancing while Jack sang a medley of Van Morrison tunes. I guess we were making quite a racket but I wasn't too concerned because for a while there things were starting to go my way.

The next day I won twenty bucks betting

on one of Jonathan Wheeler's football cards. And the following week, when Mort cracked Jonathan's gambling network, fifteen guys were put on probation but two or three of us were inexplicably overlooked. Almost every afternoon Jane and I met during free periods. The more I saw her, the more I liked her. She didn't fit into the East Coast prep school mold. Whereas most of the Cornwall girls dressed like hippies, L.L. Beanians, wealthy Parisians, or a combination thereof, Jane dressed, well, differently. Her ankle-length black coat looked more like something my grandmother would wear. And Jane didn't own a pair of Levis. She always wore funny-looking, creaseless gray pants. I'd never seen anything as ugly. But on Jane they looked great.

She was a natural. Not braided armpits natural, but home-made jam, clean, and healthy natural, an honest-to-goodness farmer's daughter. She was so unpretentious you couldn't help but feel like a phony. Jane Weston was the most beautiful girl I'd ever seen, and yet the thing I was fascinated by is hard to describe. I didn't even think about hosing her, I was just happy to be near.

The next Saturday afternoon I smuggled two six-packs and a pint of Peppermint Schnapps up to the Girls School, and, after twice hiding from women on horseback, Jane led me deep into the woods to a "fort" that she'd built during her freshman year. It was mid-November, and the leaves that had lit up the Berkshires a few weeks earlier had fallen and were a dull, crispy brown. The bare trees and marbled sky were smeared a milky-gray and the temperature had dipped into the mid-thir-ties. Most of the birds had already packed up and flown south for the winter. The only sounds were an occasional twig suc-cumbing to gravity or the caw of a procrastinating crow crying out for directions.

The plywood roof of the fort had caved in so we sat on it and leaned against a fat oak that acted as one of the fort's walls. After an hour of toking and drinking, we were both getting there.

"You know, Dunph, you're kind of a strange agent," Jane

said and then sucked on the joint she'd appeared to be studying moments earlier.

"Oh, Jeezes," I groaned. "She gets a little buzz on and starts spewing insults. Typical."

"I mean, I mean, I didn't mean that. I meant . . . you're *different* from most of the guys at Cornwall. I don't know, I guess it's because you ain't rich and you grew up in the city. Every once in a while the tough guy in you shows through."

I stood up. "I'll be right back. Mr. Tough Guy has to go wee-wee."

When I returned to the fort, Jane was examining a moth that was perched upon her coat sleeve.

"How do you like my pet butterfly?" she asked.

"Wow, that's a pretty one," I said. "You're lucky. My old man would never let me have a butterfly. Everyone on my block had one except me."

"That's too bad, Dunph."

"One time when I was about nine a stray butterfly followed me home from school—a big orange one—but," I sighed, "wouldn't you know he goes and drops a huge load on the parlor rug. Out the door." From my sitting position I performed an imaginary dropkick.

Jane put her head against my shoulder and began to laugh.

"Real funny," I said. "You didn't have to bring him to the Pound the next day."

She looked at me affectionately. It became a staring contest. I should have reached over and kissed her right then, but I choked. The silence grew awkward and I looked away. Jane bailed me out by getting up to go to the bathroom.

I gave myself a pep talk, determined not to blow the next

opportunity. I downed two or three slugs of Schnapps and took a deep breath. When Jane headed back toward the fort, I stood and leaned against one of the spongy plywood walls. She walked up to me so that our toes were touching. We gazed into each other's eyes again, only this time we locked onto something more comfortable. Jane looked happy but somehow a sad whimper squeaked out of her. She kissed my cheek. Then she dropped her head. I couldn't believe how beautiful she looked. My heart was thumping so violently I could feel my eardrums banging away. I kissed her on the mouth. Not a sloppy, wet, passionate kiss but a slow, cautious one. I tried holding my breath for as long as possible; partly because I was panting like a pervert but mostly because I was afraid that if I released my lips I'd never feel this good again.

Later that evening, Jack, Waltham, myself, and a few guys who lived on Jack's hall snuck out of our rooms and hiked up the mountain to camp out. I learned two important lessons: First of all, that I didn't know tiddly-shit about camping in the mountains, and secondly, that those guys did.

I'd heard everybody talking and, still pumped from my evening with Jane, I grabbed a blanket off my bed and joined the movement. Little did I know that each of the other guys had $250 down sleeping bags geared for moonlike temperatures which could be folded into the approximate size of a deck of cards. Thirty degrees feels like thirty below when you lie still for a few minutes in a jean jacket and a tattered blanket. I froze my grapes off and ended up throwing wood onto the fire all night just to survive.

I woke everyone at five, and in the pre-dawn light we marched quietly back to campus. At the morning assembly, our names were called and we were ordered to report to the back of the auditorium. For some reason Funderburk had instigated a 3 A.M. bed check. Because of the unusually large number of offenders and the calm, seemingly rational disposition that Fundy exhibited that day, it seemed as if commuted sentences were in order. When we were hit with nine hours each, Jack commented on Fundy's highly suspect sexual preference and received an additional three hours for insubordination.

After Fundy had left, I pointed at Jack and said, "You better watch your mouth around that guy. I guarantee that his *bite* is worse than his *bark*."

Jack smiled and said, "We'll see about that."

It was on the third day I was working off the hours that S.D. Stuart hurried up to me and asked if I had any pot.

"No," I said, "but I got some primo heroin."

"I'm serious, Tim. Find some drugs and some liquor and we'll go up in the mountains and get stinko."

I adjusted my hat and looked at her funny. "Stinko?"

"I know that doesn't sound like me but I'm not *me* any more," she said. "I've changed. I want to start having fun now."

She moved close and put her peeling, pink fingers around my gloves. Her face was bloated and pale, and she wasn't wearing makeup. "Please, Tim, I want to go up in the mountains with everybody."

"Okay," I said. "I can't go anywhere right now but I'd love to do something this weekend. We'll go to lunch or something."

"No! I don't want to go to lunch. I'm sick of lunch. I'm sick of eating; I don't eat any more. Come on, let's go somewhere."

She began pulling me away. At this point the other hour-boys stopped working and just stared. I walked her around the side of a building and said, "Listen, S.D., I'd love to do something with you but I can't right now. Fundy'll be back any minute."

"What about later?" she said. "At 5 o'clock."

S.D. looked like hell, and I was slightly afraid for her.

"Meet me behind the chapel at 5 and we'll go play," she said.

"You'll miss the last bus up to the Girls School."

"So?"

"You don't want to have to walk all the way up the hill tonight."

"I don't care, Tim, it doesn't affect me. I'm like the toughest person in the world now. Nothing affects me anymore. So you'll come out? Please say you will. *Please.*"

"Sure," I said.

S.D. hugged and thanked me and said she'd always love me. For the rest of the afternoon I was in a daze. Waltham came by, and I told him about it. He advised me to be careful, figuring Funderburk and Mort were behind it. That would've made sense but somehow I knew they weren't.

"Is it possible she's pulling an Ebenezer Scrooge and has seen the Ghost of Christmas Past?"

"Perhaps," Waltham said, "but I doubt it."

After I was done with work, I changed clothes and snuck out behind the chapel. S.D. wasn't there. I sat against the chapel wall wishing it were Jane I was waiting for. The sky was clear except for a few wispy purple clouds in front of where the sun had just set. A sliver of moon and one bright star were pinned to the cold blue to my right. Every once in a while I heard boys' voices coming from the woods. Kids smoking cigarettes or pot. That was a disappointment since these woods were only a couple of hundred yards deep. It was surrounded by athletic fields and teachers' homes, which were protected by barking dogs. We'd have to cross the fields to the mountains if we wanted to be alone. Why be alone though? I decided we could do whatever we were going to do right in these woods.

Vern Stevens and Seth Crawford came walking around the corner. "We're next," Stevens said.

"What?"

"You're after us," said Crawford.

"I'm after you what?"

Stevens looked at Crawford. "Told you we should've waited." Then to me, *"We're* next."

"What are you guys talking about?"

"You're here to meet S.D. Stuart, right?" Stevens said.

I paused. "Yeah."

"Well, we are, too. Only we've got her before you. You're getting sloppy sevenths."

"Huh?"

"You heard about S.D. in the North Dorm today, right?"

"I didn't hear nothing."

"She walked into the North Dorm this afternoon," Crawford said, "and blew five guys." The two of them looked positively giddy.

"You're crazy," I said. "Who told you that?"

"Ten guys who watched," Stevens said.

"They're full of shit," I said. "No way. She'd have to be out of her mind."

"Maybe she's come to her senses," Crawford said.

"It's our lucky day," said Stevens.

"Ain't my lucky day."

"Why the hell not?" Stevens said. "If she wants to give it out."

"She don't want to give it out. I know her. She wouldn't."

"What do you think it was, a mass hallucination?" Stevens said. "And what are you doing here?"

"She wanted to talk to me."

Stevens coughed up a laugh. "You think Crane and Kelliher are in there *talking to her?*"

I remembered the voices and turned toward the woods. Crawford grabbed my arm. I swung him against the chapel wall. "Don't touch me," I said.

"Relax," Stevens said. "You're getting all tense, Dunphy."

"Don't fucking touch me," I said.

"Okay," Stevens said, "you were here first."

When I was about thirty feet down the path, Crawford called, "Don't take your sweet-ass time in there!" I passed

Crane and Kelliher halfway in. They were flushed, nervous. "Dunphy," Crane said, "you'd better get her out of there before we all get caught. She's crazy. I don't know what happened, we didn't give her anything."

"Just get out of here," I said.

They ran.

I found S.D. laying on her side in a trampled clearing. Her clothes were scattered evenly around her, like some kind of satanic circle. Crimson goose bumps speckled her raw behind. It looked like she might be sleeping.

"Who is it?" she asked without turning.

"It's me. Tim."

"Hi, Tim. Tim Dunph. Hello, Tim Dunph. Which do you like better, Tim or Dunph? Or Tim Dunph? Or Timothy?"

"Never thought about it," I said.

"I like Dunph best. I'm going to call you that from now on." She rolled onto her back. "Are you going to fuck me, Dunph?"

"Get dressed," I said. "I'll help you back to your dorm."

She held out her arms. "Lie on top of me."

"Come on, S.D., you're fucked-up."

"No, I'm not. Why do you say that?"

I shook her ankle. "Let's get out of here."

"Why? I like it here."

"Please," I said, "you don't sound good."

"I'm all right! You're the one who's not all right but you think I'm screwed up because you're screwed up and I'm acting like you."

I picked up S.D.'s clothes and dropped them on her stomach.

"You asshole!" she said. "You can't handle it because *I'm* the one who wants it."

Her tits were larger than I'd thought. Fuller. Her bush also seemed huge, and the matted hairs were brown and wet.

"You better get dressed or you'll catch a cold," I said.

"Colds don't bother me any more. I don't get colds."

I knelt and arranged the clothes over her chest and crotch. She smelled of sweat and rubber and semen. "Yeah, you will."

"No, I won't," she said softly.

"Okay, you won't, but you'll get in trouble if they find out you're not up at the Girls School."

"I had an abortion, Dunph."

I didn't say anything.

"Did you know that?"

I shook my head.

"I did. He made me have an abortion and then he wouldn't talk to me. You want to know why? Do you want to know why he wouldn't talk to me?" She started crying. "Because he said he could never go out with a girl who'd had an abortion."

She covered her eyes and let out a deep whine. I didn't know what to say. How could I explain to her that Jonathan Wheeler was simply one of the biggest assholes alive? I touched her face and she pulled me down. She put her arms around me. The clothing on her slipped away. She felt bony and her skin cold and prickly. I warmed her back by rubbing my hands across it. Then I warmed her sides and her tits. She pulled me tighter and put her mouth to mine and when I touched her thigh she opened her legs. I rubbed her crotch; the wetness stung my middle finger at the nail. I knew I should stop but I couldn't and when I buried my face in her neck she reached for my belt buckle and I felt as lonely as I did every time I beat off. Her neck smelled sweaty and the woods were dark, the shadows blending in, and I was far from home and hungry and dirty and a little sick and I thought of Jackie and the old man and my mother and Jane, and finally I said, "No, S.D."

I gathered her clothes and helped her dress.

"I wet my pants," she said.

She pulled my hand to her wet pant leg.

We passed Stevens and Crawford and two other guys on the way to the infirmary. They looked scared and ran when they saw she was sobbing.

There was only one nurse on. I told her that S.D. needed clean pants and possibly first aid. The nurse took her into a room and came back telling me not to worry, S.D. would be taken care of and what was my name.

That's when I ran, too.

PART *Five*

On my first night home for Christmas vacation I grabbed a bus up to Suicide and drank at the Hilltop Cafe with DeCenz, Drugs Delaney, and Tommy the Wire. It was the first time we'd been out together since Mousy's funeral, and we were all feeling shitty. To make things worse, the Wire had just returned from his cousin's cornball wedding. He'd never been accused of being a hopeless romantic and the ceremony had been planned by his cousin's fruitcake fiancée, an ex-heroin addict, born-again Christian who'd left her brains in San Francisco.

"Tell you one thing," the Wire said, "if I ever get hitched, it ain't gonna be one of these make-up-your-own-poems-do-it-yourself jobs. That kind of crap's for Delaney."

I looked for Drugs's reaction, but he was on drugs and just smiled into space.

"Drugs can climb a mountain at sunrise and stick petunias up everyone's ass," the Wire said. "When I get married, it's gonna be 'I do, she dooz, let's party.' And if my wife has to leave her guru at home, well, that's just gonna be too bad."

He slammed his bandaged hand on the table.

"What happened?" I asked.

"I don't want to talk about it," he said, looking up at the Bruins game on the tube. "Every time I think of it I get more pissed off."

"Think of what?"

The Wire banged his empty glass on the table and filled it up from the pitcher.

"You know that mutt they keep inside the gate by the power lines?" he said.

"The one they put there because of your brother," DeCenz said.

"Yeah."

"Well, he's always barking and snapping at—"

"Hold it," I said. "You mean the big one that looks like an albino German shepherd?"

"Yeah," the Wire said, "the white bastard."

"That mutt *never* barks at me," I said.

"Forget about it. He never *used* to bark. The last six months or so something's been chapping his ass real bad. Anyway, I walk by him every day on my way home from school with my hands covering my ears because he's *always* barking at me. So one day I come along with a skull-busting headache, and I wasn't in no mood for his shit. So I go, '*Come on,* buddy, would you *please* shut up,' and he keeps barking, so I go to myself, 'I'll fix this mutt.' He's standing right behind the fence, you know. It's one of those wooden ones with the pointy tops."

I nodded.

"So he keeps barking with his snout pressed right up against the fence and 'POW!!!' "—the Wire uncorked an imaginary right jab—"I punched him right in the nose. I mean I *cracked* the prick. Right on the beak."

"But you busted—"

"Hey," Drugs said, "you guys ever notice how the floor in here is half tiles and half cement?"

"But you busted your hand on the fence?" I said.

"No," the Wire said. "My wrist got stuck and the cock-sucker lunges at me and rips a slab of pork out of my hand."

"He even had to get a tennis shot," Drugs said, momentarily returning to earth.

"You deserved it," DeCenz said.

"I know, it was stupid," said the Wire. "I should've just shot the prick."

DeCenz looked at me. "You believe this guy? Goes around beating up dogs for barking at him. He's gonna be great with kids."

We drank a few more beers, and then I did exactly what I'd promised myself not to do. When I slipped and mentioned Jane, I felt embarrassed so I said, "You wouldn't believe this chick's bod."

"How's her helmet?" DeCenz asked.

"Incredible. Prettiest girl in the school."

"How's her toilet?" the Wire asked.

"Perfect," I said. "Great ass."

"Big floats?" Drugs asked.

"No, but nice ones."

"She rich?" asked the Wire.

"I don't know," I said. "Probably. I'm telling you, the girl shits Twinkies."

"So what's the scoop?" DeCenz asked. "You banging her?"

"No," I said. I almost added "not yet" but I felt bad for having mentioned that she had a great body. "To tell you the truth, I don't even care if I bang her."

"Whooooa!" the Wire said. "I take it she gives some pretty nifty skull, eh?"

"No, she don't blow. I mean, you know, I don't want her to."

"What, you got the drip?"

"No, I don't got the drip. It's just that I don't even think about sex when I'm with her. Doesn't matter."

The Wire and Drugs exchanged confused glances.

"I like her," I said.

"What do you mean, 'It don't matter'?" the Wire asked.

"I mean I like her a lot. You can treat her like a guy."

"You mean she's not just a cunt?" the Wire said.

"No. She's a good shit."

Drugs smiled. "Sounds like a cool mule."

After dropping the Wire and Drugs off and making sure that Drugs didn't pass out on his steps and freeze to death, DeCenz drove to my house, cut the engine, and torched up a bone.

"Hey, Dunph."

"Mmm?"

"I been thinking."

"Yeah?"

"If there really *is* a God and all that stuff . . . do you think Mousy went to heaven after all the sick shit he used to do?"

"I guess. I mean, he wasn't all *that* sick."

"Yeah, I know, but . . . come on, Dunph, he could be pretty sick."

"What are you talking about?"

"What am I talking about? How about when he stuck the salute up that cat's ass?"

"It was already dead," I said.

"All right then, what about when he used to waste all them pigeons with his pellet gun? I mean, that stuff couldn't have gone over too big upstairs, you know?"

"Aw, that's nothing," I said, "Mousy's all set. He was a kid then. I don't think a rational God would throw a guy in hell for eternity just because he happened to have the misfortune of growing up in Pawtucket, do you?"

DeCenz didn't respond.

"What do you want, DeCenz, everyone in Rhody's pretty much the same. If He sent Mousy to hell, He'd have to send the whole fucking state."

DeCenz groaned.

"Will you please cut it out," I said. "Kids out in the boonies are snuffing out frogs left and right. I've heard of rednecks yanking turtles right out of their shells. You know what that's like?"

DeCenz looked pained. "Like getting pulled out from under your fingernails?"

"Exactly. Only worse. Anyway, it just goes to show you that everyone's a product of their environment. Mousy couldn't help where he was born."

DeCenz nodded.

"And what about when he tried to save that tree from getting cut down?" I said. "That's got to be big stuff upstairs."

"Yeah, right," he said. "Besides, maybe he'll get lucky. Maybe after you die there's just, you know . . . nothing."

.   .   .

DeCenz and I continued talking about current events that concerned us. Who was going to win Super Bowl IX, did U.F.O.s really exist, and where was the most strategic location to avoid fallout when the nuclear war came. As I was getting out of the car, I said, "We're still hitting 'Zona this June no matter what, right?"

DeCenz gave me the thumbs up. "Is a frog's ass water-proof?"

Quietly we began to sing: "I don't want to live in the city no more/I don't want to die in a nuclear war/I just want to go to a far-away shore/And live like an ape man."

When I shut the door, DeCenz goosed his engine, screeched away, and headed at the pole that had wasted Mousy. I cringed, but he swerved away at the last instant.

Never did much in the way of celebrating Christmas around my house, but that year was by far the worst. It was just the old man and me. Jackie didn't come home. To wake up Christmas Day without him there was weird.

The old man and I called the clinic to wish Jackie a merry Christmas, but the nurse who answered said he was staying with a friend of his named Charlie and she didn't know the phone number. "Well get off your big ass and find it," the old man told her. "Listen, sister, I didn't waste five bucks just to hear your fat voice."

When we reached Jackie, he sounded happier than he'd been in a while. I said, "Do the people in Arizona celebrate

Christmas like they do around here, with all the lights and shit?"

"Oh, yeah," he said. "But these people ain't from Arizona, they're from Vermont."

"Well, where you staying?"

"At their other house. They keep one here in Arizona so Charlie don't got to live at the clinic." He lowered his voice. "I think they got bucks."

"Must be nice."

"Sucks," he whispered. "His parents are sort of a pain-in-the-ass. I mean, they're friendly and stuff, but nobody wants to live at home and have to commute."

"No?"

"You kidding? Of course not. My place is frigging great."

"Really?"

"Oh yeah. You wouldn't believe all the Christmas parties we've had lately."

"Well you ain't missing nothing here," I said.

"How's the tree?"

"What tree?"

"Come on. Not even a fake?"

"You were the one who always picked out the tree."

The old man took the phone and spoke to Jackie about maybe going out to visit him. After he hung up, he looked at me and said, "Merry Christmas from your brother."

The next day I visited Bunny Cote at a local drugstore where she worked as a cashier. I wanted to talk to her about Mousy's accident. Unfortunately, the store was mobbed and

Bunny was having trouble with the cash register, so she told me to come by her house later.

"Where do you live?" I asked.

"Pollet Av."

"Where's that?"

"I don't know. I'm wicked sucky with directions."

"Do your best."

"Okay, my street's the one just past that phone booth."

"What phone booth?"

"You know, the one by McDonald's."

"All right," I said, "a phone booth near a McDonald's. That narrows it down to the planet earth."

"Right off Broad Street. Listen, I can't shoot the shit right now. Just come by here later if you want to talk."

I returned at nine, and Bunny told me all she knew. Tommy the Wire said she'd been milking it for all it was worth. Mousy had picked her up at work. She said that he'd seemed depressed. "He wasn't hisself," she said. "Like he was axing me all these weird questions."

"Like what?"

"Like, you know, religion stuff and spacey shit."

They spent the evening sitting in Mousy's car at the Hilltop parking lot "listening to Ziggy Stardust and fooling around." At 3 A.M. Mousy was preparing to make a left turn in front of my house when something caught his eye. A small shiny object in the parking lot half a block away.

"I knew it wasn't nothing," Bunny said, "but Mouse thought it was a diamond or something."

"A diamond?"

"Yeah. We were both real stoned."

Mousy switched off his blinker, drove through the intersection, and turned into the parking lot. Kicking on his high beams, he was bummed to see that his "diamond" was a Pepsi can. He pulled a quick U-ey, fishtailed out of the lot, and hit the pole.

"It was really weird," Bunny said. "Almost as if like the pole was sucking us into it. The pigs said that the tire come off when we hit, but it felt like it come off before we ever come near it."

As I was leaving the pharmacy, Bunny said, "Ain't it a kick in the pants, though. Kid would've had it made."

"What do you mean?"

"You know, he had a job at one of those power plants, he was moving to Jersey, his uncle was getting him a trailer to live in, things were really looking up."

DeCenz and I spent New Year's Eve at the Hilltop. Shorty the bartender gave us each a free shot at the stroke. Whoopee. We ended up on the watertower with a bottle of Boone's Farm apple wine. I lay on my stomach and put my ear to the icy metal. DeCenz stood at the edge, the toes of his boots protruding into side-sui-land. He gazed down, fearless. It was pointless to ask him to be careful.

"I was up here with Mousy the night he bit it," DeCenz said. "I was yelling at him, telling him to get his shit together. You should've seen him, he looked nervous. Never joked about his suicide no more, neither."

I rolled onto my back. The sky was cloudy and black.

"It's like he felt it coming," DeCenz said. He turned but stayed at the edge. "You think he felt it coming?"

"Probably, in a way."

DeCenz walked across the tower, stepping over me. "Do you think Mousy's better off dead than totally paralyzed, Dunph. I mean like the guy in the iron lung?"

"I guess."

He came back and stood over me. "You know what I been thinking? I been thinking that Mousy's probably better off dead than working for that company."

I tried to picture a nuclear power plant.

"Know what I mean, Dunph? He changed so much those last few months, it was like he died back in August. He just died. I tell you, sometimes I think he's better off this way. You think he's better off this way?"

The first thing I noticed at school in January was the heater in my room; it was on. Everywhere I went there was heat. The second thing I noticed was the food; it was good. Major improvement since the fall. The meat was identifiable, and there was plenty of it. I found out what the deal was when I was in Billy-Fu Sodani's room about to get high. I was jamming a wet towel under the door to lock in the smoke when Billy-Fu said, "Relax, friend, you don't got to bother weeth it."

This guy is really burnt, I thought. He'd already been accepted early admission at Princeton and had more to lose than almost anyone on campus. Yet here he was, still dealing, still getting high in his own room, practically running a clinic on how to get booted. I continued to line the door with towels.

Billy-Fu lit a bowl of hash. "Dunphy, would you blease cool down and pring you ass over here. No need to woory, nobody going to bust us."

His recklessness was annoying. Especially since I was only taking the mildest precautions. "How can you be so sure?"

Billy-Fu smiled. "Trust me, friend. There is no way ad-meenistration going to step feet in this room. That you can make sure of."

Finally, I suppose just to shut me up, Billy-Fu explained. Mr. Sodani, the oil minister, desperately wanted his son, the junkie, to attend Princeton. He knew that Billy-Fu's acceptance was contingent upon his graduating from C.A. He was also certain that his son would find a way to get booted. Being accepted at Princeton wasn't a cause to mellow out, it was an excuse to party. Old man Sodani knew that better than anyone. That's why he pledged five million dollars to the Friends of Austerity Fund. One million had already been received; the balance was to be presented at Billy-Fu's graduation. And that was why Dean Mort had instructed all teachers to overlook everything except murder as far as Billy-Fu Sodani was concerned.

I spent that winter getting stoned and listening to Irving's stereo. Steely Dan, Quicksilver, Boz Scaggs, Lou Reed, Seatrain, Allman Brothers, Andy Pratt, and Springsteen over and over. I didn't study much. Occasionally Jonathan Wheeler would leave his smut-filled room and cross the hall to bother me with the news of his latest coup. Being a member of the student council, he had authority to enter any room he wanted, and because Irving's stereo was one of the best in the school, I couldn't discourage him from hanging out in ours.

One Sunday morning after chapel I was toasting up a bone when Wheeler and Candle entered my room each carrying a tray. Wheeler placed his on Irving's desk and began shaking a frightening amount of Tabasco sauce into a pitcher of Bloody Mary. An eight-inch stogey dangled from his mouth. I quickly shut the door and returned a wet towel to the base of it. Candle stood at my desk, gobbing spoonfuls of mustard and horserad-ish into a bowl of tuna fish. He was wearing a sweaty T-shirt that read: "Do a mouse a favor. Eat a pussy." Wheeler handed me an album by Rudy Ray Moore. The cover pictured Rudy Ray lying naked amongst three fat naked black women. It was entitled *Eat Out More Often*.

"Hope you like your bloodys with heat," Wheeler said, and then: "Put that on."

I obeyed, and Rudy Ray began screaming out profanity. Wheeler filled three mugs and tossed in what looked like freeze-dried limes. They inflated in the drinks. I took a sip and broke into a sweat.

"So tell me, Dunphy," he said, while ceremoniously wiping and placing things back on the tray like a priest straightening up the altar after communion, "what did you think of FART's latest?"

Candle stood beside him, his left hand digging into his tuna fra diavalo sandwich, his right index finger buried two knuck-les deep into his right nostril.

"Very creative," I said.

FART stood for the Fight Against Racial Tranquility. It had gained instant recognition three days earlier when Wheeler released a stinkbomb in the dining hall during dinner. He'd then sent an anonymous letter to the school newspaper stating that "FART takes credit for the odor that permeated the dining hall on the day that has become known as 'Gas Thursday.'" Strange thing was, he didn't even intend for FART to be an affront to blacks, Orientals, Hispanics, Arabs, or any other minority. He just enjoyed being controversial. There were only eight or nine blacks in the school, and a couple of them had helped him out.

Wheeler and Candle hung around for about an hour sucking down bloodys and listening to Rudy Ray. At about one, Irving got back to the room so I tried to escape. Wheeler followed me out to the hall.

"Hey, Dunphy," he said, "are you interested in furthering mankind while simultaneously returning crackhood to its lowly rank in the hierarchy of humanity?"

"No."

Wheeler grabbed me by the shoulder and stared me down.

"I'm organizing a Legalize Rape Movement," he said. "You want in?"

I pushed him away and walked off.

Wheeler said, "What are you, pussy-whipped?"

"Fuck off."

"Okay, sucker," he called down the stairwell, "I'm not going to ask you twice, but don't blame me when your future crack takes you to the bank and back in divorce court. It happened to my father three times!"

I walked down the stairs, pushed through two sets of doors, and stepped outside. I stood buttoning my jacket in the bright sun.

"You may be Mr. Liberal right now, Dunphy," Wheeler yelled from the window above, "but wait until you don't have Weston's crack at your disposal! *Then* you'll wish you'd supported an androcentric society and fucked the Uncle Tom act!"

I was amazed that even he could be carrying this thing so far. "What if I told you that I *don't* have Jane at my disposal?" I said, immediately regretting it.

"In that case, I vastly overrated your intentions and your brains, Dunphy, and furthermore my offer is officially rescinded."

I turned up my collar and walked into town.

"Are you high again?" Jane asked while we were thumbing to New Milford.

"I have a little buzz on."

"Why do you smoke so much?"

"Because I like it?" I guessed.

"But can't we ever do something straight some time?"

I thought this over, "Yeah, I guess we could."

We ended up in a little cafe called the Connecticut Yankee. The place was run by an old lady named Joan and her twenty-five-year-old son, Billy. Joan was a nightmare. Every time her son would stop and talk to us for more than a second, she'd be all over his ass. Billy looked a little embarrassed but he kept on smiling and didn't speak back. I felt bad and considered offering him a bone but I didn't want to piss Jane off.

"Since when has my getting gooed bothered you so much?"
I asked.

"Since you started doing it all the time. Can't you go one
day without smoking pot?"

"Sure."

"Have you ever done acid before?" she asked.

"Once I tripped with my friend Drugs Delaney but I lost
him and ended up having a five-hour conversation with an air
conditioner."

"What did you talk about?"

"Oh, this and that. The air conditioner was doing most of
the talking."

The next day I received a letter from Drugs. This one got
to me easily, seeing as how my name was written on the envelope at least ten times accompanied by assorted threats and
hexes on any unauthorized readers.

> Greetings Dunph—
>
> What's happening? I hope you get this before the head
> dick because if you don't, expect a grand jury because
> we'll be fucked.
>
> Sit down before you read any more standing.
>
> Are you sitting? Okay man, you're not going to be-
> lieve this. You know what DeCenzo did? He killed
> Mousy. I shit you not. He confessed to me the other night
> that he did it. He said that you guys figured that Mousy is
> better off dead than working in New Jersey so he took the
> lugnuts off Mousy's car and the tire come off and Mousy

hit the pole and he got wasted. He said he done it because Mousy would've wanted him to do it. He did it when Mousy was parking with Bunny Cote except he didn't know she was in the car because she was going down on Mousy. That's why DeCenzo is been taking Bunny out now. Not just because she blows, I mean, but because he feels like shit about almost killing her too. Can you believe it man? Holy fucking shit! I been feeling wacked out like a bastard. DeCenzo says you woulda of done it if he didn't of did it. That ain't true, right?

Don't tell a word of this to DeCenzo because I told him on my mother's soul I wouldn't tell you till he did.

Drugs

P.S.—Destruct this letter and pretend I never told you nothing.

Waltham came running into the room

sweating and out of breath.

"Mort came looking for you in the library," he gasped, hands on his knees. "Said he wants to see *you*, Wheeler, and Creech in—" he tried to catch his breath "—his office in five minutes."

"He say why?"

"No, but it's definitely trouble."

Waltham and I ran across the hall to Wheeler's room. Candle informed us he was in the can "sawing one off."

The Cornwall cans. I put them in the same league as the Providence Train Station's men's room. A nightmare. And due to Wheeler and Candle's presence, our hallway's can was the worst on campus. The floors were always puddled, the sinks lined with stubble, and since Christmas vacation there'd been a kielbasa damming up the throne on the far left. Wheeler used to peek in periodically just hoping that all the toilets would be occupied so he'd have an excuse to piss in the sink. And there were no doors on the stalls. I think this was an alternative to saltpeter. You'd be sitting there and someone would be standing three feet in front of you brushing his teeth. And worse, when you were brushing your teeth you'd have some animal behind you, grunting.

We found Wheeler nestled in one of the stalls, studying *The Wall Street Journal.* Before I could manage a word, Waltham frantically outlined the situation.

"All right," Wheeler said, sticking his face back in the newspaper. *"Don't* get hysterical, girls. Just tell the sniveling idiot I'll be down to see him in fifteen minutes."

Waltham looked to me for help. I shrugged.

"But he wants to see you now!" Waltham cried.

Wheeler turned a page. "Well, *Irving,* presently there is an excruciatingly knobby turd dangling from my anus. So he'll just have to wait."

When we entered Mort's dimly lit office twenty-five minutes later (it took Wheeler a while to brief Creature on what we could expect), Mort looked at his watch and announced, "You're twenty-one minutes tardy—as usual."

The little light came from a lamp on Mort's desk. Only one of its two bulbs worked. The shadow of the blown one loomed like a cobra's head on the lamp shade. We sat in three straight-backed wooden chairs. The smell of pipe tobacco and books filled the room. Mort sat rigid, staring each of us down. A long list of offenses lay before him. Finally, he stood and looked out the window at the dark soccer field.

"How old are you boys?"

"Seventeen, sir," Wheeler said.

"Seventeen, sir," I said.

"I'm a couple years older," Creature said.

Mort turned his head so that he could see us out of one eye. "That wasn't the question."

"Uh, nineteen, uh, and a half."

I lowered my head and smiled. Mort spun and slammed his hands on the desk.

"I've been informed by several excellent sources—Mr. Funderburk included—that you are the three rogues who have been perpetrating this recent rash of ghastly hoaxes."

"That's a crock," I said.

"Hold it now," Mort said, pointing at me and Creature. "I know that you two may not be directly responsible but I'm also quite certain that you've been abetting Wheeler here"—he had a nervous tic when he said that name—"every step of the way. So I've news for you, Dunphy. You're guilty of complicity. I've also received information that Mr. Wheeler here is responsible for the school's rash of racial terror." Mort wore a look of satisfaction, as if he was telling us something the rest of the world didn't already know. "So tell me, Wheeler, how does it feel to be an accused racist?"

Jonathan Wheeler stared at Mort without showing any sign of remorse. He even yawned. He did a fairly good job of concealing it, but the bloodless, flaring nostrils gave him away.

"Am I boring you?" Mort asked.

"No sir," he said. "Not in the least."

We were each put on probation and stung twelve hours. Furthermore, our parents and advisors were to be notified in writing of our offenses, and these offenses would be added to our "permanent files."

The next day Jane and I hitched back to the Connecticut Yankee. We pretended not to listen as the owner Joan called her son Billy a "snivelling bloodsucker."

"What *really* bugs me about this whole thing," I said, "besides being innocent and all, is the fact that somebody went out of his way to go to Mort with this info. There's no loyalty at this fucking place. Everybody's a backstabber."

"Yeah, I know."

"How can you stand it?"

"Not much I can do about it," she said.

"That's what bugs me more. There's a bunch of assholes around here."

"You know, Dunph, if you clip a baby duck's wings before it has any feathers, the duck'll never be able to fly. I don't know the exact aerodynamics of it, but the wings just never grow the way they're supposed to. But if you wait until a duck's already grown and *then* clip its wings, the duck's only temporarily grounded. In a couple months his wings grow back, and he can fly off to bigger and better ponds."

"What the hell does that mean?"

"You're lucky," she said. "You had an opportunity to grow before you came to Cornwall and got your wings sheared off. Most of those other guys went to pre-prep schools and joints like that before they came here. They had their feathers snipped before they'd even had a chance to fly. Those guys'll never be able to enjoy life the way you will because they'll always be grounded by their own narrow-mindedness."

"Still, I shouldn't have to work hours for something I didn't do. Besides, I don't want people to associate me with Jonathan Wheeler. The guy's a motherfucker."

"Can't you get your advisor to talk to the Dean?" Jane asked.

"No way. My advisor's a space case."

"So what? It's his responsibility to defend you."

"That's irrelevant, your honor. Mr. Cole can't deal on a practical level. It'd be too traumatic for the guy."

"I'll go with you. We'll ease into him."

"Jane, you can't ease into a brick wall."

That afternoon Jane dragged me to Cole's apartment. He was on one of his highly combustible born-again highs. I expected as much. From what I'd been told, he was always either high as a kite or stuffed in a straitjacket somewhere in western Mass.

"As your advisor, it behooves me to instruct you to clean up your act and let this recent matter pass . . . *but,*" Cole said with a drugged smile, "as your friend and confidante, I say, 'Go get 'em, Timothy!' "

"Okay," I said and took Jane's arm.

She wouldn't budge. "Mr. Cole," she said, "go get who?"

"Everyone!" he exclaimed. "Tim can win over the rest of the administration in the same ticklish manner he's won me. Capture their hearts!"

"But what's the point?" Jane asked. "He didn't do anything."

"The point is this, young lady: Take advantage of the connections available to you here. Do you realize that Mr. Mort *and* Mr. Funderburk are alumni of Brown University. They could get Timothy into that school at the drop of a hat if they wanted."

"But I don't want to go to college," I said.

Cole grabbed a rag and started browsing through his bookshelf, dusting off random selections. I thought he was searching for a text to quote from but gradually I realized he was just spacing out. I've heard lithium does that to you.

I cleared my throat.

Cole looked surprised to see us standing behind him. Then he smiled. "So you don't want to go to college? Well that could change quickly. You see, contrary to popular belief, Timothy, Mr. Mort is *not* impervious to reason. Talk to him. Work for him. *Help* him. You'd be surprised at how many of your fellow students do. And those are the ones who get good recommendations."

"But I don't need a good recommendation."

"My *final* advice to you is to simply stay away from those other incorrigibles—every last one of them."

Jane said, "You're not even lis—"

"Now get out there and knock 'em dead!" Cole exclaimed. "*You* can make a difference."

He practically plowed us to the door. "Remember, Timothy," he said, "*today* is the first day of the rest of your life."

I started working off the hours on the second day of the rest of my life. Funderburk had Wheeler, Creature, myself, and most of the other hour-boys chipping ice off the walks. Jack

Rafferty was also working hours (for skipping class), but he just strolled around sprinkling an occasional handful of salt here and there and doing as he pleased.

When Fundy was off making his rounds, Wheeler called Jack over. "Hey, why the fuck do you get the pussy job?" he asked.

"Because I wrenched my back lifting yesterday."

"You don't expect me to believe that, do you, Rafferty?"

"I don't give two shits what *you* believe," he said. "I've got Fundy believing it."

As the trimester drew to a close, the pressure mounted and everyone started growing restless. Most of us were on probation, and it was becoming increasingly difficult to find a safe place to unwind. Two weeks before spring vacation, Jackie wrote me that the old man and Patty were on their way out to Arizona. Jack, Waltham, Jane, and I immediately forged parental permission slips and applied for passes to go home the following weekend.

That Saturday I made a set of directions for the guys, then Jane and I hitchhiked to my house. She almost didn't make it. She wanted to go and I wanted her along, but Jack and Irving didn't want a girl around to cramp their style. When I explained what the feeling was, Jane said, "Come on, Dunph, don't be a jerk. I promise I won't say anything."

As Jane and I hitched closer to Pawtucket, I realized that I was a little ashamed to show where I lived. Jane didn't concern me, she knew what to expect. Jack and Irving were in for a mild culture shock. The only whirlpool they were going to find in my house was in the toilet, if they were lucky enough to find it working. The old man had purchased the place in 1957 for nine thousand frogpelts. Their parents had cars that cost that much. And the old man probably couldn't get more than nine for it today—furnished.

At the outskirts of the city I started growing very tense. All I could picture was the fluorescent pink triple-decker next door. Another house on the block was sloshed aqua-blue and another orange. It's not just that my neighborhood didn't harmonize with nature; it didn't *have* any nature. The city had lined my street with baby elms in the late sixties but some gearhead sheared through every last one, like a slalom skier turning and twisting between gatelike telephone poles. The *Pawtucket Times* called him "The Midnight Lumberjack."

By the time Jane and I got there, I was sick. Things looked worse than I'd remembered. There wasn't even a blade of *brown* grass on my six-by-eight-foot front yard. One Popsicle-stick shrub twisted out of the soapy dirt like some animal's pitiful gravemarker. Chalky dog turds broke up the dusty monotony from chain-link fence to chain-link fence. And there was a brand new sign on the billboard over my house. "Give the United Way," it said, and it pictured a little boy in a wheelchair.

Jack Rafferty was a real scream. He asked if the Dunphy house was an "hysterical landmark." I was sort of relieved that he'd come right out with it, though, and I even laughed when he said that the inside smelled "like centuries of chicken soup" because it did. Jane tried to be more gracious. "This is great," she said enthusiastically, "your next-door neighbor's only ten feet away. I have to walk about two miles to visit my nearest neighbor back home."

That night I phoned a bunch of guys and told them to round up a party. It was the first time in years that my friends entered the house. They'd made it a point to avoid the old man. By nine-thirty things were progressing well except the guy/girl ratio was running five to one. I was at the kitchen table with Jane when DeCenz stuck his head out of my bedroom and said, "What happened to your trees, Dunph?"

"Had to get rid of them," I said. "They were getting too big."

Years earlier I'd tried to grow a couple potted trees in my bedroom. No matter how much attention I gave the droopy bastards, they refused to grow. It was like trying to get a palm tree to take root in Siberia. Some plants grow through cracks in the sidewalk, but even with chemicals and nutrients and loving care mine wouldn't budge. The problem was that my bedroom window was in an alley and the sun only managed to flicker in for about six minutes a day—half that in winter. Eventually I gave their skeletons to my Aunt Dot because she had a huge picture window. When I visited her six months later, the trees looked like they'd been dipped in glue and rolled in grass clippings. They were about seven feet high and four feet wide.

Waltham introduced himself to Drugs Delaney and flashed his bag of weed as a sort of calling card. Irving had recently fallen grease-backed head over wing-tipped heels for a Westchester, New York, girl named Kara Kellinan. She was a junior at the Girls School and was heavily into cosmic awareness and drugs. Irving Waltham was the kind of guy who associated James Dean with pork sausages. In order to get into Kara's

ballpark, he'd bought an oz. of high-altitude Colombian rain-
bow weed off Billy-Fu the night before we went to my house.
He'd then nailed the door shut and sat in our room for hours
playing with his pot. He weighed it, cleaned it, weighed it
again, then sat at his desk rolling and re-rolling bones. He tried
several techniques and timed himself at each.

Drugs Delaney was the perfect mentor. Ripped jeans, a red
flannel shirt, a rope belt, long hair pulled back in a ponytail, a
sparse, random beard like metal slivers on a magnet, and a
feather earring. He'd recently traded in his VW microbus with
the bumper sticker that read SUPPORT THE MARINES for an old
Volvo with WARNING: I BRAKE FOR HALLUCINATIONS. He never
went anywhere without his idiot dog, Roachclip. Someone had
accidentally given Roachclip some bad acid when he was a pup
and they were sleeping outside the Providence Civic Center
waiting for Dead tickets to go on sale. The poor dog had been
walking into walls ever since. Drugs was lucky; he'd eaten the
same acid but got sick on a bottle of Jack and puked most of it
up.

"What kind of weed is this?" Drugs asked after lighting up
and taking his first toke.

"Marijuana," Irving replied.

Jane and I laughed. Drugs looked at us quizzically and
then also laughed.

"Hey, that's a good one, Herbie," he said.

"Irving," Waltham corrected with an awed smile.

Drugs Delaney had already eaten his Vitamin Q's
(Quaaludes) and was well on his way to achieving cerebral
paralysis. He'd done two hits of blotter acid the day before, so
tonight he was taking it easy.

"This is good shit," Drugs said. "How much it set you back, man?"

"Pardon me?" Irving said.

"How much did it cost, Irv?" I said.

"Three sawbones," he answered.

"Bucks," I whispered. *"Sawbucks."*

I told Jane that I thought we were cramping Irv's style so we went into the parlor where Tommy the Wire was confiding to the world about having recently knocked up his girlfriend, Debbie Sylvia.

"So what's her beef?" Jack asked. "Hasn't she heard of women's lib? Chickens pay for their own abortions these days."

"Right on," a guy named Mickey Costa said, raising a clenched fist.

"Yeah," the Wire said, "but the thing is, this bitch is *all* fucked up. First she says she wants an abortion, then she wants the kid, then she wants to have the kid and just dump him in an orphan joint, and now she wants the abortion again. Dumb-shit'll probably end up having the abortion and keeping the kid anyway."

"T.W., are you *certain* you planted the seed?" Jack asked.

"Yeah," the Wire said proudly. "She don't screw no one but me. Like one night I tried to talk her into blowing Costa while I porked her up the ass, you know, just to prove her love to me, but she wouldn't go for it."

Jack frowned. "Prude."

"Yeah," the Wire said, "she's a little old-fashion so I told her to forget it. I said she didn't have to blow no one except me if'n she didn't want to."

Jane nudged me and said, "Who said chivalry is dead?"

At eleven o'clock two carloads of women arrived led by Bunny Cote. The Wire pointed her out to Jack and said, "There's another one with a major social disease."

"Which one?" Jack asked.

"Bunny. The one with the big floats."

"I mean which social disease?"

"Same one," the Wire said. "She's pumped up. Pregnant as they come."

Jack looked at me and said, "Introduce me to Bunny, Dunph."

"Why?" Jane asked. "You heard the Wire. She's pregnant."

"Exactly," Jack said, craning to get a better look. "No reason to hold back now."

I looked for Jane's reaction.

"Don't worry, Dunph," she said. "I'm not saying a word."

When Bunny plowed her swollen breasts near us, I introduced her to Jack and Jane.

"That's a nice camel-skin sweater," Jack said.

Bunny looked around the room. "It ain't camel-skin," she said, absent-mindedly. "I think it's polyester."

Jack felt her sleeve. "Jesus, you're absolutely correct. I noticed the humps and just *assumed. . . ."*

"Hey, Dunphy," Bunny said, "you seen DeCenz anywhere?"

Before I could answer, Jack took Bunny by the arm. "I told him I'd meet him in the other room," he said. "Come on, let's track that fucker down."

Jack led her straight into the old man's bedroom. He shut the door and the lock clicked. It gave me a funny feeling, my old man's bedroom and all.

Jane followed me into my bedroom. I locked the door. She stood in the middle of the room examining the pictures and posters that my brother had hung on our walls. There was a poster of two hippos humping with a Make Love, Not War slogan, and another of two pigs fucking beneath a Makin' Bacon sign. There were old Red Sox players like Joe Foy and Mike Ryan and Jim Lonborg on my door and a "Carl Yastrzemski For President" sticker on the lamp shade.

Jane pointed to a framed picture of a farm surrounded by mountains. "Is that a real place?" she asked.

I squinted as if I'd never seen it before and walked past Jane, purposely smashing my head on the picture. "Uh, no," I said, "I guess it's just a picture."

She frowned. "I meant does that place really exist somewhere?"

"Yeah," I said, massaging my nose. "I'm sure it exists *somewhere*. I don't know, probably someplace in Arizona. That's what I always figured, anyway."

Jane stayed in the middle of the room and cupped her elbows. I sat on my bed, but she didn't join me.

"Why do they call that guy 'Tommy the Wire'?" she asked. "Did he used to be real skinny?"

"No. His name's Tommy Dwyer and everyone pronounced it Tommy de Wire and, I don't know, it just became Tommy the Wire."

Both of us knew that this was it. Jane was pretty open-minded but she'd refused to consummate things in a church, railroad yard, junkyard, or cafe. Those were the places we'd been forced to resort to for privacy. I got up and kissed her, then pulled her down on the bed so that we were laying on our sides, facing each other. Put my hand on her chest and she began breathing heavier. I slid a leg between hers and tried to unfasten her belt, but her hand was clenched over the buckle.

"You got a good defense," I said.

We kissed again for a couple minutes, and when we seemed to be reaching some kind of mutual crescendo, I tried to cram my hand down her pants. She grabbed my wrist.

"What's the matter?" I asked.

"Nothing. I'd just like to keep my pants buckled."

"Well why didn't you just say so? I'll buckle them right back up after I get them off, silly."

I felt for the metal clasp again.

"Please, Dunph, I don't want to."

"Why not?"

"Because I like the position we're in now. Come on, cut it out."

"All right," I groaned.

Then I kissed her. Passionately. Jane was the one who finally stopped it.

"Duuh-unph."

"What, I can't kiss you anymore?"

"The kissing's fine, but what do you call this?"

Meaning why was I humping her leg.

"It's a nervous tic," I said.

Jane smiled and kissed me. I took it as an invitation, but again she intercepted my hand. "No, *seriously.* Cut it out."

"Why?"

"Because I can't."

"What do you mean, 'because you can't'?"

I suddenly thought I understood. "Are you on the . . . uh . . . bad time of month?"

"No, that's not it."

"Well?"

Jane sighed. "I just can't."

"Listen, if you're worried about getting pregnant, you can relax. I've been spayed."

"Hey, Dunph," she said, "how can I have a relationship with you if you're never open with me? You don't take anything seriously, and it kind of scares me. I don't think you've ever been serious with me for more than thirty seconds. Sometimes I feel like I don't even know you. You never tell me nothing personal."

I knew she was right, but I was in a tough spot. I was in love with Jane and wanted her badly, but I didn't dare tell her that—on account of Mousy Town. He'd always said that the quickest way to get dumped on was to inform a girl that you love her. "Soon as you do," he said, "they got you by the grapes and it's only a matter of hours before they start squeezing." Mousy said that affection was a weakness that women instinctively exploited. I felt that Jane could be an exception, but I didn't want to take any chances.

"I still don't exactly know why you want to move to Arizona," Jane said. "I assume it's got something to do with your brother, but you never explain. And like you've never once mentioned your mother."

"I haven't mentioned the Holocaust either," I said.

"But it's just that you *never* get serious. You don't confront things, like the thing with Mort and your advisor."

"So?"

"So you don't improve anything. You bitch about it but you don't do nothing. You've got to get more involved. Speak up."

"Jane, would you please blow me?"

She rolled over.

"I'm *kidding*," I said. "I just don't know what you want from me."

"Obviously."

We lay there waiting for the mood to blow over. It didn't.

"Listen, Jane, ever since I met you I've treated you like my best friend. I never hurt you or lied to you or fucked you over, have I?"

"No."

"And these guys plan a 'weekend with the boys' trip, but I take you along."

"You're a saint."

"I didn't say that. I'm saying just the opposite. You see, if I didn't take you along I'd have a lousy time myself. In a way I'm using you because my life's dull when you're not around. You're the funnest person I know. Just sitting here talking to the back of your head is a blast. You're really the greatest, Jane, and I guess I take advantage of that. But you know I'd never use you for sex. You know I wouldn't. So do I have to come right out and say it?"

WAS pulling off her panties when there was a knock on my bedroom door.

"Hey, Dunph," someone said with a laugh, "you better get out here. Your buddy Herbie's pretty fucked up."

"You stay here and start warming up," I said to Jane.

"What?"

"I mean, you know, start warming up the bed."

I quickly dressed and went to check on Waltham. He was staggering around the parlor with a loony grin, carrying an empty quart bottle of tequila and wearing a doily on his head. He'd already knocked over a lamp and was singing "99 Bottles of Beer." Everyone was laughing at him but somehow I heard Tommy the Wire above the throng say, "At least he's got a semi!" That's when I noticed Waltham's drunken pecker peeking out of his fly. Jane came up behind me laughing.

Amidst a round of boos, I led Waltham into my bedroom and sat him on my bed. I pulled the tequila bottle out of his hand. I could've broken it over his head.

"You're killing me, Irv," I said.

He just smiled.

"How much of this bottle did you drink?"

"None of it," he said.

"Irrviiinnng? Come on now. Don't bullshit me."

"I thwear, Dump. I jutht drank the thtuff that wath inthide the bottle."

Jane broke up again and said, "Cripes, Dunph, he sounds like you when he's drunk."

Irving noticed Jane for the first time.

"Don't worry about me, Mrs. Dump. I took a buncha . . . vitamin Qs 'fore I had 'sing to drink."

I should've figured. If Drugs Delaney would feed his dog acid, then why not pump Irving Waltham with Quaaludes?

Waltham begged me to let him return to the party, so I followed him into the parlor and kept a watchful eye. I figured after seventeen years of milk and cookies he deserved a night like this. He ended up drinking out of a beer can that Drugs was using as an ashtray. Remarkably, though, he hung in there and at 4 A.M. he waved and slobbered a drunken goodbye upon the last few guests.

Bunny was the last to leave. She was swearing at Jack as he followed her to the door. She wasn't too happy with me, either.

"Dunphy, your friend here's a snake," she said. "I don't know what the hell you told him but the crum's been terrorizing me all night. What do you take me for, a fucking hooer?"

Jack looked amused. "Jesus, Mary, and Joseph, Buns—"

"Don't call me Buns, you sleazebag!"

Bunny burst out crying, ran down the steps, and crossed the street. I caught up to her at her Vega, parked beside Mousy's pole. She was sniffling and fumbling with her keys at the door. "Bunny, wait a second."

"Fuck you! I don't need your shit. I know you never liked me none anyhow." She got the door open. "You think you're pretty smart and everyone else is stupid, but you got a lot to learn 'cause you don't know nothing."

I didn't say anything, and Bunny stood there wiping her eyes.

"It's almost like you blame me for killing Mouse except you

ain't even liked me before that. You act like I got no right to hang out with you guys. You know, I spent more time with Mouse last summer than anyone. Why can't you believe that I really loved him? You know what I think? I think you guys never really loved him yourself 'cause if you did, you'd understand."

"I do understand," I said. "And I like you."

"You got a funny way of showing it, throwing me out of your house last year at 3 P.M. in the morning. You want to know something? I cried when I got home that night because I thought you was such a nice guy before. No wonder you don't get along with Pop. He's real people."

"I get along with Pop all right."

"He thinks you hate his guts. I told him I met you and he goes, 'Yeah, he's a good kid except he hates my guts.' I couldn't believe it. I says, 'Your own son?' "

"I don't fucking hate his guts."

"Maybe not, but he thinks so. Just like you might not hate me but I think you do. I wouldn't leave my worst enemy with that sleazebag you fixed me up with."

"Listen, he usually ain't such a bad guy. He must be drunk."

"That's no excuse for what he was doing. That guy's a creep, and you can't convince me different."

"I'm sorry."

Bunny had stopped crying. "I'd like to know what you told him."

"I didn't tell him nothing," I said.

"Oh, fuck off." Bunny climbed into the car and rolled

down the window. "Just take my advice and be more careful who you hang out with." She started the engine.

"Drive carefully," I said.

"Maybe I will, maybe I won't. I don't need you to tell me what to do."

She stepped on the gas a few times, throwing exhaust all around me.

"You know, Dunph, sometimes I pray for you. I do. Because I think that deep down inside you're probably a nice guy. You just got to learn to show it more."

She rolled up the window and drove off. I stood there until her car blended in with the rest of the city's groans.

When I got back inside, Jane said, "Sounds like Jack made a friend for life."

"I don't know what her prob is," Jack said.

"What'd you do to her?" I asked.

Jack put his arms around Jane and me, and said, "Nothing that an intelligent chicken wouldn't have loved."

When the horizon hinted at dawn, Jack persuaded DeCenz to take him up to the water tower. They'd been talking about our Arizona plans, and Jack wanted to be sworn in as a partner. I stayed at the house positioning Waltham's head while he assaulted the toilet bowl. By the time I got to bed, Jane had started her period.

The next afternoon Drugs and DeCenz picked us up in DeCenz's father's Monte Carlo, and we drove back to Cornwall. We hadn't gone five blocks when Drugs said, "Ut-oh, man. I forgot my squeef at Dunph's house." We turned around and passed a familiar pillow case lying on the side of the street.

"Oh, wow, man," Drugs said, "I think I left Dunph's shit on the roof."

"You spaceshot," I said.

"Hey, that's gratitude for you," Drugs said. "You never would've found it if'n I didn't forget my squeef, man."

"He's right," Jane said. "Give Drugs credit. At least he's consistent."

We set out for a second time, and DeCenz suggested we stop at the Hilltop and pick up a case. You couldn't legally purchase beer on Sundays in Rhode Island, but Shorty sold it under the counter. While I was in the Hilltop, Drugs began twisting up the bones, and by the time we got out of Pawtucket, we were all (with the possible exception of Waltham) baked. Irving's face emitted a pukish green hue while Jack recounted his previous night's antics.

"How could you let me?" he groaned.

"Believe me, Irv," I said, "we didn't let you. If we'd *let* you, you would've woken up married, tattooed, enlisted, and *dead.*"

"And I actually dropped trou?"

"Well, no," Jack said, "you didn't actually *drop* them. But your little nuts were dangling out of your zipper. Man, you are hung like a wild field mouse."

"I wouldn't worry about it," Jane said. "At least you had a semi."

PART *Six*

When spring vacation arrived, I didn't go home. The old man had received Mort's letter, and I didn't want to give him an aneurysm by showing up so soon after. The Dean implicated me in every atrocity that Jonathan Wheeler ever thought of. I stayed at DeCenz's house for two days and then thumbed down south and met Jane at the Woodstock, Virginia, bus station. Her mother dropped her off there thinking she was going to visit her roommate Brooke in Sarasota. Together we hitched to Key West, then back up to Lauderdale, then we cut across Alligator Alley and cruised up the Gulf Coast.

We fucked for the first time in a horse field in Four Oaks, North Carolina. Jane liked to call it "making love" but I didn't. A couple of my friends' ex-girlfriends had used the term with an embarrassing smugness that gave me the creeps. Mousy Town said the phrase was introduced just so Catholic girls could start fucking and Jewish girls could start having orgasms.

After that morning in North Carolina, we fucked every chance we got. I wanted to use a rubber but Jane didn't like them.

"They take the spontaneity out of it," she said. "We'll have to stop every time for you to put one on."

I frowned.

"Seriously, you don't have to worry about it," she promised. "I'm like a clock. Every twenty-eighth morning at 8 A.M. We'll just have to cool off on the fourteenth day for a few hours. And I'll go on the pill when I get home."

When we were in Key West, I said, "Just for the record, Miss Timex, what happens if you *do* get pumped up?" I was hoping that Jane had nothing against abortions.

"Don't worry," she said, "I'd take care of it."

"I wouldn't let you go through it alone," I said. "I mean, you know, I'd help out, too."

"You're *such* a gentleman."

I loved those ten days we spent down south. The girl was like a drug that made me feel great about myself. I felt good about the outline of my knobby knees in my baggy pants or my toes sticking out of the holes in my sneakers. I liked it *better* if I had a lopsided case of bedhead or if my eyes were swollen from just awakening or even if my pants were slung halfway down the crack of my ass. I felt more comfortable with Jane than I'd ever felt with anyone. Naturally she took advantage of that.

" 'Ja ever play with yourself, Dunph?" Jane asked one late afternoon as I was lying on my back in shorts and a T-shirt on a deserted beach in Naples, Florida. She was sitting beside me, her smooth, tanned wheels crossed Indian-style, reading a *Cosmopolitan* issue that she'd plucked out of a garbage can. We both were wearing gangster hats I'd stolen from a *Guys and Dolls* production at school.

"It says here that ninety-nine percent of all teenage guys beat it."

I lifted the felt brim and looked around to make sure no one had snuck up on us. Jane's nose was buried in the magazine.

"Well it must be true if it says it in the distinguished medical journal, *Cosmo,*" I said. "But let me tell you something, Jane." She finally looked at me. *"Playboy Magazine* claims that eighty-six percent of all teenage girls occasionally get kinky in the carrot patch—solo, if you know what I mean."

I arched my eyebrows.

"So you're saying you do masturbate?"

"Well . . . I *have.*"

"Wow. That's intense."

"What, you don't think every guy beats off?"

"I mean intense that you'd admit it to me."

She smiled. "Did you beat off the first time you got a boner?"

"Of course not. I've been popping woodies since I was in my mother's womb. There, we finally brought my mother into a conversation."

"You think married people masturbate?"

"No." Then I thought about it. "Jesus, I hope not. That'd be pretty pathetic."

We only had fifty dollars between us for the whole time so we slept out on the beaches. A couple nights we were chased out of little towns on the Gulf Coast by the local oinkers, but mostly people left us alone and it never rained once. We ate French fries and hot dogs and fried shrimp at greasy shacks along the road, and we fished off the pier for our dinner when we got to Naples. The last two days, when we'd blown all our dough, we chewed and screwed from three Howard Johnson's. It was the best time of my life.

An almost-full-moon sat in the night sky

like a lopsided softball when I returned to Pawtucket. The thick smell of pizza and cigar smoke seemed to rise out of the cracks in the pavement. I'd called DeCenz from Providence and told him to meet me at the Hilltop, but I had trouble catching a ride and didn't get there for over an hour. The laughter of men echoed across the parking lot.

DeCenz wasn't in the bar, but Shorty the bartender said that someone in the corner booth wanted to talk to me. The man had his back to us.

"Who is it?" I asked.

"Someone," said Shorty.

My old man was staring at his martini. I knew I was slunkmeat.

"Well, if it ain't Beach Blanket Bingo," he said.

"What are you doing here?"

"What the hell you think I'm doing here?"

"Drinking?"

"I'm waiting for you, Dildo."

"How'd you know I was gonna be here?"

"I stopped in and your buddy DeSenseless told me you was on your way. You want to have a glass of loud-mouth soup with your old man?"

I sat across from him.

The old man called Shorty by his name and held up his martini. "Two more," he said.

"You know Shorty?"

" 'Course."

"I didn't know that."

He smiled. "There's a lot you don't know about your old man."

It sounded like a threat.

"So what's the story? You running away from home or what?"

"Went to Florida," I said.

"I know you went to Florida. I don't care if you want to go to Florida, Jesus, *everyone* wants to go to Florida, but don't you think you could tell your old man what you're doing? What, you're a hot shit all of a sudden? You don't tell me what you're doing no more?"

"Thought you were pissed at me."

"I *am* pissed at you. For running down to *kagotz* without telling me."

"I thought you were pissed before that, though."

"For what?"

"Didn't you get a letter from Mort?"

"What, you think I'm gonna believe that cocksucking bastard? I raised you better than that, Dildo. Your Mr. Mort's gonna have *two* broke hands the next time he lies about any kid of mine. I knew you ain't done none of that shit he said. They can't fool the guy who raised you."

"Hold it," I said. "Are you telling me that Caveech was the one who broke Mort's arm?"

"I got nothing to do with it. Your old man's a straight shooter. Had nothing to do with you neither. They owed Caveech money. You're lucky you got in when you did, though, because now he's all paid up and the school don't want nothing to do with him. For Christ sakes, Caveech couldn't get one of them genius Japs in there if his life depended on it."

Shorty brought the drinks all the way over to the booth, something I'd never seen him do for anyone.

"This your first martini?" the old man asked.

"No." I downed it in one gulp. "We used to do martini shooters."

"Holy shit."

I wanted to order another immediately. Didn't feel comfortable with this man-to-man stuff.

"I'll always back you up when you're right, Dildo. I always told your teachers they could give you a backhand if you ever got out of line—and I believe in that—but I never told no one they could smack you for no reason."

"I appreciated that."

"Listen, wiseguy, the family always comes first with me," he said. "Anything I ever done was for the family. Remember that. The family comes first."

I nodded.

"You don't believe me, do you?"

I looked around uncomfortably.

"You always think I'm out to screw you or I'm lying to you," he said. "You think it's my fault that your blessed mother killed herself."

"I never said that."

"But you never said nothing. You think it, though. Let me tell you something. God knows I tried to help your mother. I was a young guy when we got married, not much older than you now. What are you, eighteen, nineteen?"

"Seventeen."

The old man smiled. "Seventeen, *madonne,* that's a great age to be. That's a great age to be. I was twenty-six when I married your mother. She was only a kid. Nineteen. I'm telling you, Dildo, you never seen such a beauty. These broads you guys hang out with, with all the shit on their face, they don't compare. Your mother, oh boy. All the time she used to get depressed, though. No matter how happy she really was, she'd still feel sad. I could give her a million frogpelts and you know what she'd do? She'd cry for three days. I couldn't never do nothing to make her happy. Took twelve years for you to come along. We'd almost gave up. Then, pow, along comes you, this wriggly little thing I didn't even recognize. I bawled my eyes out the night you was born. I thought everything would be good." He stopped and stared at his drink again. "Want another martini?"

"Guess I'll just have a beer," I said.

"Shorty," the old man called, "a beer for Dildo." He pointed to me and everyone at the bar laughed.

"Pop, do me a favor. Don't call me that unless we're at home."

"What?"

"Dildo," I whispered.

"I always call you Dildo. It's a joke."

"Yeah, so what does that make me?"

"Oh Jesus, what's the matter, you think your old man don't love you no more? Come here, give your old man a hug."

"Pop, come on."

"What, are you afraid to hug your old man?"

"I'll give you a hug at home."

The old man's eyes filled up.

"I was like you once," he said. "It's too bad. It's really a shame. I never hugged my old man either." He looked around the room and shook his head. "You remember him at all?"

"Not really."

The old man smiled. "Boy, he was crazy about you. I wish you could've known him. *That* was a man."

"I seen pictures."

"Pictures ain't nothing. It's like you'll show your kids a picture of me some day and it won't mean nothing to them. They'll never know how mean your old man was to send you to a great school and work his tail off six days a week so he could raise you and your brother to be good kids and not end up on the street or in jail like all the guys your mean old man grew up with."

Shorty delivered the beer.

"You remember your old man, Shorty?" the old man asked.

"You kidding?" Shorty said. "Greatest man who ever walked the face of the earth. Used to beat my ass in if I got out of line, though. What a hook he had."

Shorty went back to the bar, and the old man said, "See? Old men are special. I know it's hard to believe, but some day you're gonna miss me. Look at Shorty."

I sipped my beer.

"You'll know how much I cared about you and your brother. You think I wanted to get rid of you two? What for? I'm gonna throw wild parties like your friends? The family's the most important thing in the world to me. You don't break up the family."

"Bullshit," I said.

The old man sat up as if a spring had busted through his seat. I took another sip.

"What?"

"I said that's bullshit."

He grabbed my wrist. "You watch your fucking mouth."

"Then stop lying to me. I'm sick of the family speech and your old man and all that shit."

I pulled my hand away. The guys at the bar were listening to us so I lowered my voice.

"I know you were divorcing Ma when she died," I said.

He stared at me for a moment and then sat back. "No," he said softly, "you don't know nothing."

"Well then tell me!" I yelled, and the guys looked over again. "I want to know."

The old man slowly stood up and took out his wallet. He threw some paper on the table and walked away. I followed him out to the lot.

"You always say I never say nothing. I'm talking now, Pop." I grabbed his arm when he tried to climb into the car. *"Pop,"* I said.

"Your mother loved you and Jackie and that's all you got to know," he said.

"Okay, just forget it. If you can't tell me everything then don't tell me nothing."

I headed back into the bar. The old man slammed the car door, and I stopped.

"Life ain't a fucking fairy tale, buddy!" he said. "I got news for you. It ain't Ozzie and Harriet, and things don't always turn out the way you want. I loved your mother, but I couldn't live with her after a while. She drove me fucking nuts, okay? That what you want to hear?"

He raked his fingers over his head and then scratched at his face.

"It was stupid to get married," he said. "We weren't made for each other, but I loved her at first sight and I was an idiot about it. I thought she'd become something she wasn't. The woman was mentally ill. She was afraid of life. She never wanted to leave the house; for God's sake she never even learned how to drive a car. It made me crazy. In almost twenty years, you know how many times we went out to dinner? *Once*. One time. On our tenth anniversary, that was it, we went to Dienno's."

The old man started to shake.

"I guess you'll never forgive me until it happens to you, huh."

I didn't answer.

"Well then I hope you never have to forgive me," he said.

I never expected the old man to break, so when he did and he hugged the roof of the car, I didn't know what to do. I just stood there, sweating and feeling a little sick to my stomach. Finally I couldn't handle it. "Jesus Christ," I said, and I walked back inside.

The next day when I was leaving to thumb back to Cornwall, the old man was in his easy chair eating out of a half gallon carton of ice cream. He was only wearing boxer shorts and one of his grapes hung out. The chair had been permanently stuck in the reclining position for years, so the old man had to climb over the arm to sit down and spread his feet to watch television. I don't know whether it was his pale legs or the vanilla around his mouth or the grape or what, but suddenly I felt bad for the guy. He looked old and I'd told him off and I wished to hell I hadn't.

"Gonna eat that whole thing?" I said.

"Just picking."

"That was full last night."

He smiled. "It's good stuff. Breyers. Supposed to have all the natural preservatives in it, none of the fake junk. Here."

He gave me a spoonful.

"That's good," I said.

"You should try this other kind they got. 'Heavenly hash.' Oh, *madonne,* you can't even get the stuff no more. I got to bribe the kid at Norm's to hide some for me." The old man laughed.

I felt like hugging him but I was weak and didn't.

"I'm taking off," I said, and I stood there.

"One thing before you go."

"Yeah?"

"That little girl you're running with."

"What about her?"

"You putting the wood to her?"

"What?"

"Don't give me that 'what' shit, you think I don't know what goes on? You listen to me. Be careful. It's the guy's responsibility as much as the girl's. Don't go getting your friend there in trouble. You kids think you can fuck everything you meet and not pay the price. Well, you can't. These poor girls, they got feelings."

"I know," I said.

"All right, you just remember that."

"I will," I said, and then I picked up my bags and left home.

That evening there was a notice on the bulletin board stating that Dean Mort wanted to see me and Waltham in his office at 10 o'clock. The Dean sat at his desk with Funderburk standing firmly over his shoulder. Mort pointed at Irving and then me and said, "Dumb. Dumber." Through a shower of tonsils and spit, he said he was aware we had taken an illegal weekend at the end of the Winter Term. Because I was already on probation, I'd have to face the Disciplinary Committee the following evening. Since it was Waltham's first major offense, he wouldn't face the D.C. but he was being put on probation.

"The baby ducks got me again," I said to Jane the next morning.

"Yeah," she said, "me too."

I felt bad for her. Though her first offense, it was a fucking doozy by Girls School standards, and she was going to have to face the Girls School Disciplinary Committee alone. Those old bags were brutal. They'd call her a whore for taking a weekend with three guys. And they demanded even more explicit details than the Boys School D.C. Are you a virgin? *Were* you a virgin prior to the weekend? Jane took the news admirably. She told me to worry about myself. She knew that if I didn't say all the right things I'd probably get bounced.

After a two-hour hearing, the D.C. decided to keep me on an in-limbo basis. In other words, if I was caught doing anything else, I'd be expelled without even the formality of another D.C. hearing. I was also tagged with a twenty-four-hour work project. Which meant my baseball career was over.

Jane's hearing lasted three and a half hours and, after finally getting her to crumble, the Girls School D.C. decided to let her remain in school under the same terms as me. Except she was hit with a thirty-six-hour work project. Furthermore, Jane and I were put on "socials," which meant we were barred from speaking to each other for the remainder of the year. If we were so much as overheard mumbling a "good morning" in passing, we'd get hit with additional hours.

Getting busted seemed like the best thing that ever happened to Waltham. He acted all bummed out but deep down inside he really loved it. It was P.R. In a matter of days, he shelved the Brylcream and decided to go with the dry look. Then he traded in the flood pants for a pair of farmer jeans and dumped the wing tips in favor of work boots. The Coke bottle Band-Aidified glasses were replaced with Coke bottle, John Lennon-style wire rims and, to complete the image, Irving canceled his *Business Week* and *Wall Street Journal* subscriptions and started reading *Rolling Stone* and *High Times*. Believe it or not, it worked. Waltham started seeing Kara Kellinan on a steady basis. I was happy for him.

About a month into the term I got a message from Jane asking that I meet her in front of the grocery store at 4:30. I ran through a downpour all the way into town. Jane was waiting outside the store under a canvas awning. She was wearing her black overcoat and gangster hat. In those eyes was a look I'd never seen before.

"What's wrong?" I asked, turning her so that her back was against the store's picture window.

"I think I'm pregnant."

I hung my head and listened to the drumming of the raindrops on the canvas. All at once, everything seemed to be conspiring against us. Jane's hands were twisted together against my chest.

"Don't look like that," I said, pulling her head to my chin. "It's no big deal."

Jane wrapped her arms around my neck like a little girl hugging her father.

"I can scrape up the money," I said. "I'll borrow it from someone. You just got to get permission to go to Boston for the weekend. Tell them you're looking at colleges or something."

She stepped slowly away. "What are you talking about?"

"You know."

"No, I don't think I do. Tell me."

"I'm talking about going to Boston."

"Why?"

"For the abortion. Where else are we going to go?"

She looked spaced-out.

"Don't worry," I said. "I'm going to."

"I'm not getting an abortion."

I waited for an explanation. Was there an easier way? Could she just take a pill or something?

"What are you saying?"

Jane's chin flushed, drew in, dimpled. "I'm having the baby. It's not that hard to figure out."

"You were the one who said you'd have an abortion!" I yelled.

"What?"

"Don't give me that innocent shit, Jane. Remember in Florida? When I asked you what you'd do if this happened?"

She blinked. "That's right. And I said I'd have the baby."

"No, no, no, no, no. Your exact words were that you'd take care of it."

Just as I was saying it, it struck me what she'd meant.

"That's right," she said. "I said I'd take care of it. The *baby,* not the *abortion,* you jerk."

I reached for Jane's hand, but she pulled away and glared at me.

"You know, you're a frappin' shit-bum," she said, suddenly hoarse.

Again I tried to touch her. She pushed me away and started crying. I felt sick. I handed her a folded-up ball of toilet paper, but she threw it in a puddle and wiped her eyes and nose with her sleeve.

"You always try to take the easy way out, don't you?" she said. "That's why you have to get stoned all the time and why you want to go out west so bad. You just can't face reality. You know, you're warped. You can't face *anything.* You're a frappin' phoney shit-bum." She wiped her nose again. "But I guess I always knew that."

Jane stepped out from under the awning and dropped her head back so that the rain washed her tears away.

"Well, at least you were honest about one thing," she said. "I guess we never did make love. You were just fucking me."

She ran back toward the school. I watched her reflection in the store window and weakly called out, "Jane, wait," but she kept running.

I stayed in front of the store, unable to convince my legs to move. It was as if my body had gone on strike. I was a fire hydrant or a "No Parking" sign. The drumming on the awning grew louder. I thought about what a motherfucker rain was. Maybe my brother wouldn't have climbed the power line had it been raining. Kennedy would've had the bullet-proof bubble up. I stared at an empty vegetable stand littered with limp leaves of lettuce. I guess I looked wacked-out because after a while some guy pulled down the shade inside.

PART *Seven*

"Go after her," Irving said. "You don't want to lose this one. Believe me, you don't want to lose her."

"It's too late," I said. "She's lost."

"It's never too late. Just tell her that you're sorry and that you need her back."

"Ain't that simple, Irv."

"Come on, Dunph. You were the one who told me I could get any girl in the world."

"Yeah, but getting them *back* is another thing. The chances decrease exponen— . . . expent— . . . You know, like in geometry."

"Now *you're* the one who sounds like a pussy."

"Don't you fucking see? What I did was unforgivable. I mean, what's she gonna tell the kid? 'Your dad wanted to pull the plug on you but I talked him out of it.'"

"She doesn't have to tell anyone anything."

"But *she'll* know," I said. "How can she marry the guy who wanted to kill her kids?"

"Hold it right there. There's never been any proof that a fetus is a living human being. You weren't going to kill a *person,* just the thought of one. Technically, everytime anyone masturbates they're killing possible life and—wait a second, did you say *marry* her?"

I was getting a headache.

"You'd actually *marry* her?"

"I don't know. I guess so."

"Holy cripes," Irving said, "I never knew anyone who got married before."

The next afternoon Irving and I hitched to the Connecticut Yankee. I thought it would feel good to go there again but it was depressing as hell. Joan was on a roll. As soon as her son Billy went into the kitchen, she came over to our table and in a conspiratorial voice said, "I think he might be a fag."

"Who?" I asked.

"Billy. I think he might be a fag."

I was horrified for Billy but had to ask, "Why do you say that?"

"Well what do you think when two men take a shower together and lock the door?"

Irving and I looked at each other and then back at Joan.

"Well it's not *conclusive*," Irving said, sympathetically.

On the way home, I said, "Can you imagine poor Billy putting up with that shit his whole life? No wonder he's a homo."

"Yes," Irving said. "That may have contributed to it."

"I'm surprised he doesn't just take off."

"I'm not really."

"Why not?"

"I don't know," Irving said, "I suppose he probably loves her. Sometimes you have no control over who you love, Dunph."

It was Saturday, May 17, three weeks to the day before graduation. At 8:30 that night Jack Rafferty sent word for Wheeler, Irving, Candle, and me to meet him in his room in fifteen minutes. Strange, but what the hell. When we were assembled, Jack unveiled three quarts of Bacardi, two dozen cans of coke, a few limes, and several bags of ice.

When we started boozing, we were hardly speaking and when anyone did speak it was a whisper. Everyone except Jack was on probation so we were forced to use extreme caution. At 10 o'clock someone got hold of a deck of cards and we began playing fifty-cent games of poker. At 10:15 the radio was flipped on, but the volume was kept very low. Jack started to turn it up, but Irving said, "Hey, take it easy, Jack. Just because you're not on pro."

By 1:30 in the morning the radio was on full blast; everyone was smoking butts; a bowl of hash was making its twentieth lap around the room; Wheeler, Creature, and Jack were swearing on their mothers' souls that they'd anted; and two empty rum bottles were lying in pieces on the pavement below the dorm.

Springsteen's "Rosalita" was pumping away when a faggy voice proclaimed, "As I live and breathe!" Even before we could register whose set of vocal cords it was, our nimble fingers were firing cigarettes around the room in a gale of sparks and ash. Funderburk was standing in the doorway, his arms folded and his face radiating satisfaction.

One by one my codefendants pleaded for mercy. Surprisingly, even Wheeler begged for another chance. Creature's plea was the most ridiculous. "Please, Fundy," he said, "my mother's gonna have a royal bird if I get bounced."

"It's *Mr. Funderburk* and why should *you* really care? You haven't attempted to gain one ounce of knowledge during the three years that you've been at C.A."

"Oh, that's bull! When I come to Cornwall I didn't know nothing. I couldn't talk good, I couldn't read good, but you guys made me read a lot of books and stuff and it really improved my . . . um . . . you know, my ummm . . . ." Creature waved his index fingers in a circle. "My uh . . . you know, uh . . . the amount of words you know."

After pathetic groveling by everyone, Fundy began to rant and rave in a nonsensical cackle. For the first time in his life he had a truly captive audience and he was inspired. The gist of his sermon was that we were all hopelessly doomed and that he resented us "enormously" because we were not law-abiding tools.

When Fundy's tirade was twenty minutes along, I got fed up. I realized that I didn't give a shit if I got booted. I had nothing to stay at Cornwall for anyway. The old man already told me that he had to work and couldn't make the graduation, Jane had dumped me, the diploma was toilet paper, so I figured the sooner the better. I didn't need a lecture from this guy.

"Excuse me," I said. Fundy didn't hear me and continued yelling.

"Excuse me," I repeated louder, but again he paid no mind.

"Hey baldy!" I yelled, immediately corralling his attention.

Fundy regarded me with amusement.

"Listen," I said, "why don't you stop bugging us. I'm sure you got better things to do than crash parties."

Fundy's head snapped back. "What's that supposed to mean, Mr. Bigshot?"

I lifted a magazine off the card table, uncovering the half-played hash pipe resting in the ashtray. I put it to my lips. Then I picked up the lighter. All eyes shifted to the pipe in disbelief.

"Oh, you little punk! Now you've done it," Fundy sang staccatolike. "Now you've *reeeaaallly* done it."

I lit the bowl.

"Dunpheeee!" he cried. "Have you lost your mind?"

It took several lights to get the moist hash to burn properly, but eventually I managed a good draw.

"Not at all," I said, without exhaling. "But if the D.C. finds out who I bought this hash off of, C.A. could lose four million frogpelts."

I exhaled, filling the room with smoke.

"What's a frogpelt?" Fundy asked.

"Money. Dollars. Four million of them."

"Why do you say that?" he asked with waning confidence.

I began cleaning out the bowl with a coat hanger. His nervousness got me pumped.

"Well, earlier tonight we purchased a large quantity of blond Lebanese hashish from a certain rich A-rab who resides on the Cornwall Academy premises. And—" I blew into the pipe *"should* our little get-together here reach the Disciplinary Committee, I'll just have to spill the beans." I began refilling the bowl. "Now you don't think the D.C. could in good conscience expel all of us without also booting that certain *Princeton-bound* A-rab, do you?"

Fundy started stammering, shifting his weight from leg to leg. Nobody spoke for about thirty seconds but Jonathan

Wheeler displayed a rare smile. I felt foolish sitting there holding up the bowl, but I'd played my hand and it was Fundy's turn to either go out or match me.

He called me "insidious" and "insolent" and "conniving" and noted that what I was attempting was "out and out blackmail." A series of teary "how dare yous" followed and he capped his speech by threatening to get me "but good" if I *ever* threatened him again.

"I'm not threatening anyone," I said, "I'm just doing my duty to ensure that all parties realize the extent of their actions."

Fundy recoiled.

"Listen," I said, "if you *still* feel that I'm being unfair then you have every right to turn around, walk down to Dean Mort's house, and tell him everything."

Fundy walked out into the hallway and then back into the room. An air of cautious optimism settled over us. Finally, he said, "Dunphy, can I have a word with you in private?"

Out in the hall, Fundy stammered before saying, "I can't believe you. You'd actually turn in one of your pals just to save your *own* skin?"

"Look, I'm really touched by your concern for our minority students but Billy-Fu's going to do okay with or without a Cornwall Academy diploma. It's those guys in the room here who'll be hurt the most."

"Okay, Dunphy, I'll make a deal with you. I'll let three out of the six go free, and I'll make certain that you're one of the three." He looked down as if he'd been far too generous.

"That's not exactly my idea of a good deal," I said.

A faint layer of tears actually washed over his eyes.

"Dunpheeeee?!" he said. "Come onnnn. You could at least have the *decency* to settle this thing in good faith. Somebody has to take the blame. It's not as if I found you five miles up in the woods. Now don't get greedy."

"Okay. Jonathan Wheeler takes the blame for everyone. The rest go free."

"What?"

"We go back in there, and you pick Wheeler's name out of a hat."

"Why Wheeler?"

"Why not?"

Fundy's panting subsided. He blinked all the moisture off his lashes and grinned.

"You just made a big mistake, Dunphy. I can tell Wheeler what you were planning, and he'll turn around and blame everything on you."

"Good. Throw me out, too."

"You don't understand. He'll blame *everything* on you. Which will leave Sodani scot-free."

"You really think Jonathan Wheeler's going to let his only hope off the hook?"

"He just might be mad enough."

"He'd get mad but he wouldn't lose his cool. He never would've lasted here this long."

Fundy knew I was right.

"As it is we're going to have a hard time getting him out," I said. "You have to get him to agree to the terms before you pick his name."

"No."

"What do you mean 'no'?"

"No. You're complicating matters. I'll grant you that only one goes, but *I choose who."*

Fundy seemed firm. I knew I'd be pressing my luck not to give in.

When we re-entered the room I knew I was being set up to be the fall guy, but I didn't care. Although Wheeler would stay, I'd at least saved some of my friends. I outlined the terms of the deal. "Fundy's going to pick one guy," I began.

"Mr. Funderburk," Fundy said.

"And whoever he picks got to promise not to involve anyone else. In other words, you brought the hash from home."

Fundy finally smiled. "Okay, do I have any volunteers?"

I started to get up.

"Sit down, Dunphy, you're not even worth throwing out."

He looked at Wheeler, Candle, and Creature. "You three aren't either," he said. "No, it's between Waltham and Rafferty." He smiled. "Now which one of you wants to be the sacrificial lamb?"

Great, I thought, all the better! Jack was the only guy in the room who could get through this without getting booted. He'd definitely get a hefty job project and be put on probation, but that was nothing compared to what anyone else would get. Unfortunately, he didn't want to be the lamb. He stared at Fundy, unblinking, his mouth closed tightly, his jaw muscles flexed. Even after Irving had left with Funderburk, Jack remained holed up in his silence. He was that way when the last of us returned to our rooms.

The rumor around campus was that
Waltham was going to be used as an example to any seniors
who may have had visions of enjoying the last three weeks. In
light of this, I asked for permission to make a short plea to the
Disciplinary Committee on his behalf. Before I spoke, Fundy
presented the school's case. The description he gave to the D.C.
was ludicrous to the point of being a caricature of Jonathan
Wheeler—never mind Irving Waltham. He called him a "mali-
cious malefactor" who was determined to "disrupt and defile
the Cornwallian way of life."

When it was my turn to speak, I basically called Fundy a
lying sack of turds. Mort immediately objected, saying, "How
dare you attempt to coerce this committee by disparaging our
colleague's unquestionable probity." Funderburk bowed in
Mort's direction and then savored the proceedings with the
subtle, smug look of a man who is beyond reproach.

Since the truth was out of the question, I decided to throw
Waltham at the mercy of the committee and simply asked for
their compassionate forgiveness and a rational punishment.
"Come on," I said, "you guys know that Irving is a good guy.
The truth of the matter is that he got spring fever and busted
loose a little. Haven't you ever done anything crazy?"

Waltham was kicked out of school that evening. I was
stunned. When I'd left the hearing, I felt he was in pretty
decent shape. Two of the D.C. members had had him in class
and said that he'd always been a polite, respectful kid. Unfortunately, hotter heads prevailed.

Saturday night I helped Waltham carry his stuff to a waiting taxi. I couldn't help but feel responsible.

"Hey, I'm really fucking sorry, Irv," I said. "If it was up to me, I'd take your place."

"Stop it," he said. "This has nothing to do with you."

"How's your old lady?"

"What do you mean?"

"How'd your mother take it?"

Waltham shrugged. "Cripes, I don't really care *how* she takes it. She didn't get bounced, I did. I hope she learns a lesson from it, though."

"What's that?"

"She better buy a lot of tuition insurance the next time she plans on running my life and locking *me* up in a hellhole like this."

We put his bags in the backseat.

"Jesus, I'm sorry," I said again.

"Don't you see what's happening, Dunph? I've *changed*. They're throwing me out because I've changed. Do you realize in the last two months I've pursued and landed the girl that I wanted, I've partied when I've wanted, I've done *everything* when I wanted. Don't you see? It's like the school's telling me that I'm *not* such a pussy after all. It's official; Irving Waltham is back."

He shook my hand and climbed into the front of the cab. After he'd shut the door, he rolled down the window and said, "Thanks for everything, Dunph."

"Thank *you,* Irv," I said. "You're a very cool guy."

I finally got the nerve to call Jane and beg her forgiveness, but she wouldn't talk to me. Her roommate told me to fuck off, Jane and I were finished. I knew it wasn't true. I'd done some major damage but I loved her and I'd tell her so and she'd smile and maybe cry again and find it in her heart to take me back.

I finally spotted Jane walking back to the bus following classes. The catwalk was choked with people moving in different directions, but I twisted through them and caught up to her. "I got to talk to you," I said.

"Write me a letter," she said and pushed past me.

I ended up walking backward all the way to the bus. She kept her head down, her hair hanging limply over those eyes, purposely blocking her view of me.

"I'm sorry," I said. "I was under pressure and lapsed back to the Pawtucket way of doing things. Please look at me. *You were right, I was a jerk.*" I bumped into the bus and continued up the steps backward. "Come on, Jane, give me a break, I swear I'll never snap like that again."

"Don't worry about it," she said, looking up with shiny, wet cheeks. "It turns out I'm not after all."

Everyone on the bus was watching her bawl. I scoured my pockets for decent tissue. I couldn't find anything but shreds so I wiped her eyes and nose with my hand.

"What do you mean 'you're not'?" I whispered. "You said you were like a clock."

"Well I must've forgotten to set my clock ahead because I'm not." She continued to sob. "Must've been nerves."

I tried to wipe her face again, but she pushed my hand and said, "Just go away. You did me a big favor. I didn't think I was ever going to get over you but now I am."

I didn't budge, just stood there wiping my brow.

"Dunphy!" Jane cried. "Please get out of here. I know what you did to S.D.!" She looked into my eyes. "I know," she said. "Jack told me everything."

As I shuffled down the aisle of the snickering bus, I heard a familiar voice say, "Domestic problems, Dunphy?" To my right, in the front row, sat a smiling Funderburk. He hugged a briefcase to his chest like a bulletproof vest. "That's five hours each," he said. "You broke Socials."

I dropped by Jack's room with a six-pack

of beer. Offered him one but he refused, saying he wasn't feeling well.

"Oh, come on," I said. "A couple beers'll be good for you. They work just like Alka Seltzer. You know, the bubbles."

"I don't have a stomachache."

"Beer's good for whatever ails you."

"There's that punster again," he said, and he gave in.

I opened the window and followed him onto the gutter.

"Jack, *why?*" I asked.

He looked nervous and lowered his head. "I couldn't help it, Dunph. I froze. I really let Irving down, didn't I?"

"Don't give me that shit, asshole. I know what you did. I just don't understand why you'd buttjam us like that."

"What are you talking about?"

"I ain't stupid, Rafferty. I know it wasn't a coincidence that Fundy stopped by the other night."

"What do you mean? We were making a fucking racket!"

"Bullshit. Fundy *always* knows when to stop by."

"So what does that have to do with me?"

"He told me everything," I lied. "Out in the hall the other night. Fundy told me everything."

Jack dropped the droopy-eyed act and bared his business-like soul. I got the creepy feeling I was watching a psycho shift gears. "They made me an offer I couldn't refuse," he explained ever so unoriginally. "Fundy and Mort promised to get me into Brown if I kept an eye on you guys."

"That's what I figured."

"Jesus, Mary, and Joseph, Dunphy, I wouldn't have lasted through winter term if those guys had wanted me out, you know that."

"But Waltham . . . ?"

"The numbers were off, and they needed somebody. He was available."

"The *numbers* were off?"

"Mort has this fucked-up quota for booting people. The trustees make him keep things strict as hell. They don't want any rabble-rousers."

"But we're talking about Irving Waltham, man. He was a fucking good student."

"I didn't want Fundy to pick Waltham but, I must admit, it didn't hurt my cause."

Jack made a show of checking out the stars. I think he was even pleased that I'd caught him. Now somebody knew how clever he'd been.

"I've seen the future, Rafferty. You're always going to be surrounded by Funderburks and Morts, guys who'll jump at the first chance to stab you in the back, just like Fundy did the other night. I saw the look on your face when he put you on the spot. He could've just picked Irving, but he didn't. He wanted to humiliate you. It's the nature of the world. You stab us, they stab you, and some bigger dick stabs them."

"Like I give a fuck about Irving Waltham."

At that instant I hated Jack Rafferty more than I ever thought I could hate anyone. I just wanted to get away from him.

"One last question," I said. "Whatever happened to the Jack Rafferty who said he wouldn't even *apply* to any Ivy League schools because he'd have to fellate too many people? When did he become a blowboy?"

"Flexibility is the key to success."

"Fool."

I opened the window and started to climb back into the room.

"You're the fool, Dunphy."

I was straddling the windowsill. "That doesn't mean much coming from a guy who fucks his own friends."

"I fucked more than that."

I leaned my face against a windowpane.

"Fucked your old chicken," he said. "I fucked Jane Weston before you even touched her."

"You're a liar."

"I fucked her good. Then I dumped her off on you."

"Fuck you," I said, but the truth made me sick to my stomach.

"I didn't expect you to believe me, you loser. You can't face facts. That's why you're going to Arizona, and I'm going to Providence."

I stepped back onto the rusty gutter, dizzy, fearless. I moved toward Rafferty, and he smirked. I slapped his face and the smirk was gone.

He spit at me.

"Jesus Christ!" he yelled when I grabbed his arm.

He gripped ahold of me, and we stood there swaying on the narrow ledge, four floors up, him scared shitless, me out of my mind. Then I thought about Irving and what he'd do in that situation, and I saw how pointless and predictable it all was and I let go of him. Jack held on for a few seconds but I didn't say anything, and when he finally released me I climbed in the window and walked away.

The next Tuesday my math teacher Dave Swanson asked me to drop by his apartment for a talk. With his sad brown eyes and easy manner, you couldn't help but like Dave. He seemed like a normal guy. Also, he was one of the few young teachers who refused to scour the countryside in search of illicit activity. Dave half-jokingly told my class that he would be more inclined to raid students' rooms but that he'd harvested an extraordinarily potent crop of his own herb that year. Because I liked him I'd worked a lot harder in his course than in my others. I didn't want him to think I was stupid.

I felt a little tense when I got to his apartment, figuring Fundy had spilt the beans. After I was seated on his musty, tapestry-covered sofa, Dave returned from the kitchen with two bottles of Miller beer. When he cracked them open and set one on the table in front of me, I slipped him a wary look.

"You drink beer, don't you?" he asked.

I peered under the table and then walked over to a closet door. I grabbed the glass doorknob and glanced suspiciously at Dave. Then I swung it open and scowled as if expecting to find Mort and Fundy crouched amongst his rugby equipment.

When I sat back down, Dave raised his beer and toasted to June 7th (Graduation Day). After five minutes of small talk, he asked me why I'd been pulling consistent As in his class when I was barely passing the rest of my courses. "Come on, Dunph," he laughed, "you're making me look bad."

I felt embarrassed and shrugged. "Luck?"

"No way," he said. He pulled out my last test paper and circled a thirty-step problem that I'd aced.

"I could've used cheat notes."

"But you didn't."

"No."

Dave watched me swig my beer. "Well?"

"I'm sorry, Dave, I'll make it a point to flunk the next couple of tests."

I gulped down the rest of my beer and stood to leave.

"Sit," he said. "I'll get you a refill."

When he returned from the kitchen, I was still standing. He handed me another Miller.

"Would you please sit down and relax?" he said. "You're making me nervous."

I sat down wondering if he really had something important to say or if he just wanted a drinking buddy.

"Mr. Cole tells me that you don't intend on going to college next year. Is that true?"

"Partially. Actually, I don't intend on going to college *any* year."

Dave seemed disturbed by that. He took butts from his top pocket, shook two or three halfway out and held the pack out to me. "You smoke?"

"Nope," I said, accepting one, "but I'm trying to start."

"You mind if I ask you a few questions?"

"Go ahead."

He paused. "Do you really know yourself?"

"What do you mean 'do I know myself'?"

"I just want you to be sure that you know what you're doing. At least consider college as an option."

"Listen, Dave, I'm not a moron."

"I'm aware of that."

"Well, trust me, college ain't for me. And I'm not going to end up any worse off on account of missing it. I read a lot. I just don't read the shit that I'm supposed to."

"What do you read?"

"You know, the *Times*. The *Providence Journal* before I came here. And since I don't like what I been reading, I don't plan on participating. It's not that I'm a radical, Dave, in fact, I'm just the opposite. I'm an ananarchist, an old-fashionist, whatever you want to call it. Let's face it, it's a strange, fucked-up world—I like normalcy. And please don't give me the 'one man can make a difference' speech because he can't and this ain't the sixties."

Dave stood in search of an ashtray. "Then what are you going to do?"

"I'm going to move out west to a nice, small town and become a human being again."

He frowned.

"Hey," I said, "is it so wrong to want to live in a place where your kids can play safely in their own backyard?"

"Oh, I get it. You're going to move to Maple Syrup, USA, marry a virginal beauty queen, raise six or seven towheads, and have the little lady bake her apple walnut crunchies for the church bazaar?"

"No, no, no, that's not it at all. Jesus, I don't even *like* virgins."

"Don't blame you," he said.

I had to smile, coming from a teacher and all.

Dave took a long drag on his butt and snapped out two perfect smoke rings that hovered above us like fading halos.

"Dunph, can I get heavy for a minute?"

"Go ahead."

He leaned forward and scratched his brow, carefully measuring his words. "How's your life been so far?"

"Not bad," I said, rolling my hand back and forth, "hot and cold. I mean, compared to whose?"

"If you could relive it, what changes would you make? What would you do differently?"

"First of all, I *wouldn't* live it over again even if I could. Not that it's been that horrible. I just don't think I could bear to listen to all the same songs, watch the same tube, see the same shit. But if I had to, I don't know . . . I guess I'd live it pretty much the same." I thought about Jane. "Maybe make one or two changes."

"What about your grades? Would you work harder in school?"

"Nah."

"Why not?"

" 'Cause I already told you, I don't plan on going to college."

Dave seemed satisfied. Maybe he was just stumped. For a few minutes the conversation changed. We made fun of Fundy. After opening two more beers, he asked what I thought of C.A. in general.

"In general," I said, "I think the place stinks."

"Don't beat around the bush."

"It sucks, blows, bites."

"There you go."

"Cornwall Academy and I are miles apart," I said. "Face it, Dave, there's something fucked-up when a psycho like Jonathan Wheeler practically runs the place and Irving Waltham gets bounced. The system's burnt."

"Ever consider that your small town plans might be sort of a cop-out?"

"*Cop-out?* Please Dave, this isn't 'The Trial of Billy Jack.' Listen, I was born a hundred years after my time. I'm sorry, but I hate plastic. I hate anything to do with modernization. Are you thrilled about the prospect of nuclear war? Well, it's gonna happen. Unless you're lucky enough to be killed in a car crash or something, someday you're gonna find hydrogen and neutron bombs flying all around you. I ain't happy about that.

And I'm not too tickled over the prospect of cobalt salt bombs, either."

"What are they?"

"I think that's what they're called. A friend of mine named Mousy Town told me about them. It's a bomb—"

"Mao-tse-Tung?"

"No, Mousy—as in rodent—Town—as in city. He told me that cobalt salt bombs are these bombs that could actually destroy the universe. I don't think they've made any yet, but the way they figure on paper is they'd cause a never-ending chain reaction of explosions. It'd blow the shit out of everything."

Dave's eyes widened, impressed; he kept nodding as if I was saying something he expected to hear. Then he said, "Be up front with me, Dunph. Do you hate your father?"

"No, I don't hate my father," I said, "and you're starting to sound like Billy Jack again. *Be up front with me.*"

"Don't you feel guilty about not working harder at Cornwall after all he did to get you in here?"

I thought about Mort's broken arm and almost laughed.

"What are you complaining about?" I said. "I'm getting all As in *your* class."

"You can't tell me that you've tried in any of your others."

"Maybe not, but I don't care about the others." I was getting a little cocked and felt argumentative. "You really want to know what I feel guilty about, Dave? I feel guilty about my little brother being paralyzed. I feel guilty because he'll always be my *little* brother. I feel guilty because I get chills up my spine and a sick, shrinking feeling in my grapes every time I see him with no clothes on. I've tried to get over it, but I still can't look at his flabby legs or his bloated, old man's belly. And maybe I'm fucked-up for even thinking about it, but I feel sick to my stomach that he can't get a hard-on."

Dave lit up a smoke and again offered me one. I declined.

"What happened to your brother?"

I reached down and took a butt without thinking. I didn't intend to be so fickle.

"Twentieth century casualty," I said. "Fell from a power line when he was ten."

"Broke his neck?"

"Well he ain't Gumby."

Dave flipped his lower lip inside out.

"Listen to me, Dunph. You can't spend your whole life worrying about yesterday. It's gone and it's not your fault; you're not God."

"So it's God's fault? I'm glad that's finally cleared up."

"You know what I mean," he said. "Don't let guilt control you. It's your life, do something with it." There was silence. "I'm sorry about your brother."

"Don't be. It's typical. My brother gets crippled, my old man sends me here, the only girl I ever loved hates me, my best friend loses it and ends up dead. My mother . . . everybody I like gets fucked." I dragged on the butt then ground it into the ashtray. "Even my teams get burnt. Barnes breaks his leg, Aparicio slips rounding third, something *always* messes up. Could've been the happiest day in history and Barnes has to break his leg." I stopped. Hadn't meant to reveal so much self-pity. And I was getting carried away. Happiest day in history?

"Go on," Dave said.

"It's not important," I said, throwing my arms down in disgust. I got the feeling that he thought I was snapping. First

Mao-tse-Tung and now Marvin Barnes. "It's just a typical example. Providence College, my favorite hoop team, was in the N.C.A.A. semis a couple years ago and they were bombing Memphis State by something like fifteen points in the first half and suddenly God looks down and sees me and my brother and *poof!* Sure as shit, our big man breaks his leg, P.C. gets trounced, and everyone forgets about us. Story of my life." I gulped my beer. "Same thing with the '72 Red Sox. Aparicio slips rounding third, we lose the final game of the season by a run, and the pennant by a half game. A *half* game."

Dave looked puzzled so I said, "That was the year of the players' strike. The schedule was all messed up."

Suddenly I noticed I was crying. The beer seemed to break down whatever had held back the tears. I couldn't recall the last time I'd managed a single drop. Not when Jackie broke his neck. Not even when Mousy died. Then I remembered. My mother was giving my brother and me a bath and Jackie was crying because the water was too hot, and I was starting to cry until my mother said, "Look at Timmy, Jackie. Timmy doesn't cry because he's a big boy," and I did stop and I was proud and I hadn't cried since. It all came out. I began hemorrhaging tears.

"I love my father," I said. "I love my father."

Dave put his arm around my shoulder and rambled on about how he'd been all bummed out too when he was graduating from high school. He said that a lot of guys bawl their eyes out at this point in their lives and that I shouldn't be afraid to love my father.

"I love him," I said again and the more I repeated it the easier it got. "God, I love him."

PART *Eight*

A mosquito dove past my ear like an ambitious fighter pilot. I listened as he looped around the darkened room and whizzed by my head again. He'd been attacking me for two hours now. Most of my fellow seniors were out celebrating their final night at Cornwall but I'd chosen to stay in. Wasn't in much of a partying mood but I felt pretty good, almost as if I'd earned something. I thought about the dumbfounded Italian guy who had once asked me how long I'd been carrying my dog's corpse. At the time I'd considered the question foolish and the man an idiot. Now I remembered him with a kind of respect. I'd been carrying one corpse or another ever since. But it was over, I was cleaning out the closet.

Final exams had been a breeze, but they generally are when you're just aiming to pass. Once again the skeeter blew past my ear. I heard a door squeak open and slam shut. Got up to see what was going on. Jonathan Wheeler was kneeling on his floor painting a message on a large linen spread before him. Candle stood behind him wearing inside-out, skid-marked underwear and a U.S. Air Force T-shirt. Skid-marked is an understatement. These things looked as if an eighteen-wheeler had locked its brakes on them at a buck ten. When Candle turned around I noticed the printing on the back of his T-shirt: "Death from Above."

It was June 6, 1975, and while the rest of the nation was

commemorating the 7th anniversary of Robert F. Kennedy's assassination, Jonathan Wheeler was kicking off his own Sirhan Sirhan celebration.

"Dunphy," Wheeler said, "you should see my new crack. Kneesocks, braided ponytail, only a sophomore, cute as a button. Know what I fucked her with the first night?"

"Jesus," I said and I turned around.

My hand was on the doorknob when we heard a thump out in the hallway. Candle cut the lights and I hid in the closet.

"Why do you hate me?" Wheeler whispered.

I didn't answer.

"You blame me for S.D. getting gang-banged?"

"No," I said. "You're just the one who pumped her up and then dumped her."

"What are you talking about? Your buddy Jack was the daddy, asshole. I never even touched her."

"No way," I said.

"Of course. He was fucking her the first week of school while you were at home planting your dead friend."

I took my chances, bolted across the hall and slipped into my room.

I sat at my desk and thought about what Wheeler had told me. Too much. Somehow I knew it was true though. Everything was turning out to be lies and misunderstandings.

Then I saw it.

At first I mistook it for a rolled-up sock. But it moved. Under my bed, looking me straight in the eye, was a mouse. Got on my hands and knees to get a better look. The mouse saw me and scampered into the closet. I crawled after him and almost died. In my closet, beside the mouse, beneath my shirts, was a pair of legs. In the dim light they looked like ape's legs. An equally furry hand reached down and scratched the ankles. That's when I heard an unmistakable sound. Whatever was hiding in my closet had just farted. I noticed a knapsack lying on the floor.

"DeCenz?"

He peered out from between my shirts. The mouse scooted out of the closet and hid back under the bed.

"Yeah, Dunph, it's me. I didn't hear you come in." He smiled. "You hear me rip one?"

"What are you doing here?" I said, holding a hand to my chest. "You scared the living shit out of me."

DeCenz picked up his bag and came out of the closet, still scratching his legs. "What do you mean, what am I doing here? I been driving all night, you could give me a better greeting than that."

I couldn't muster one, though, and luckily DeCenz sneezed.

"I just died," he said.

"What?"

"I just died. Whenever you sneeze, your heart stops and you die for a second."

"Really?"

"Yeah, that's why you bless people when they sneeze. 'Cause they were just dead." He pulled a bag of weed out of his top pocket. "Got any papers?"

"No," I said. "I quit smoking."

"Why'd you do that for?"

"I'm gonna take the summer off. No pot, no booze—except for weekends I'll drink a little beer, and on Thursdays."

"You're crazy, man. We're going to the tequila capital of the world and—"

"I'm not going to Arizona," I blurted.

"What you talking about?"

No reply.

"Dunph, don't give me this, man. We're going, right?"

I looked at him and he knew I wasn't.

DeCenz gawked at me for a second and then threw down his bag. "I *knew* this would happen," he said. "I fucking knew it."

"Things change."

"Things change all right. You know you're jamming me?"

"What, am I ruining your getaway?"

"Dunph," DeCenz whined, "don't do this. We're going. I got to go."

"Give me a break."

"You gonna fuck Jack too?"

"I don't think Jack's going," I said.

"God, I can't believe what a traitor you are."

"You got it wrong, DeCenz. If I were a traitor, I'd go."

"Oh yeah, right. So what are you gonna do, hang out in Providence and go to Reject like every other dumb fuck?"

He sat on my bed and sulked. "Okay," he said, "I'm gonna blow your mind. There's something I been meaning to tell you." He drew a deep breath and said, "I wasted Mousy."

"Is that right?"

"Is that right? What the fuck, is that right! I tell him I killed—is that right, he says."

"You killed him?"

"Yeah. I loosened the tire on his car. I did it because one of us had to and you wouldn't. Did it for his own damn good."

"You murdered Mousy for his own damn good?"

"He was sick, Dunph. You know that."

"Sick? He makes a decision on how he wants to live his life and because you disagree, he's sick? When did you become a fucking guidance counselor? I mean, who the hell are you?"

"A friend, that's who."

"You know, DeCenz, this is exactly what's messed me up my whole life: worrying about other people's decisions. Well, I'm through with it. I can't help it that my mother killed herself, and I can't help it that Mousy wanted to work for a power plant. I can't help those things, and I'm not gonna worry about them any more. I'm just gonna worry about things I can do something about. That's what Mousy was really saying. Remember the tree that got cut down? Mousy was trying to teach us a lesson. Face up to your problems, DeCenz. Do what you can do while you can do something."

I turned and looked out the window. "Go back to Pawtucket. Listen to your conscience for once."

"I can't go back now," he said.

"Because of Mousy?"

He shrugged.

"Cut the shit," I said. "I know you didn't kill nobody. You're making the crime fit the accident."

"Who says?"

"*I* say. You'd have to be a fucking homicidal maniac to try it with Bunny in the car."

"Listen, Columbo, maybe I didn't know she was there. You ever think of that?"

"Are you telling me that you thought that by loosening the tire you could get Mousy to drive his car into a telephone pole and kill himself? Come on, it doesn't make sense. You already said that you had him up on the water tower with you earlier that night. Why didn't you just push him off? Would've been a hell of a lot more practical. No way, DeCenz, you couldn't hurt a mosquito and you know it."

"Look, man, we planned to go to Arizona and I'm going. I'm the only one who does what I say I'm gonna do."

"Don't go, it'll be another mistake."

"A mistake? Everything I do is a mistake. Tell me, what the hell's not a mistake?"

"No wonder you worried about Mousy going to hell," I said. "You're just like everyone else in Pawtucket, you don't give a damn. When we talked about going to Arizona, it was because Mousy thought we could have a fresh start there, away from Pawtucket. Only you wouldn't be starting fresh, you'd be taking the city with you! Don't you see? Your change wouldn't be mental, just environmental." I sat beside him on the bed. "Listen, you're eighteen years old, and you made a mistake. Everyone makes mistakes. But not everyone admits them."

"You know what I did, Dunph?"

"What?"

"I got Bunny pregnant. And she's having it."

"That's what I figured."

"That's what you figured. That's what *everyone* figures. Great, so what do I do? I ain't even sure it's mine. I only banged her a few times."

"Whose else would it be?"

DeCenz thought about this.

"All right, so what am I gonna do?"

"Just do the right thing. You didn't murder nobody, you just got a girl pregnant. And she needs you now, so help her out. Bunny's a lot sharper than you think."

"So what do you mean? I should marry her?"

"Christ, no. Not if you don't want to. But I know one thing, you should own up to it and give her support. How do you think she feels, the poor kid? Be nice to her, DeCenz. She's a good shit."

While DeCenz was working it out in his head I shut up and moved to the window.

"I can't believe this," he finally said.

"What?"

"Me having a kid."

We looked at each other and laughed.

For about an hour we talked about Bunny and what DeCenz should do. Wasn't all that tricky. I convinced him to drive back to Pawtucket that night, before word spread that he'd run.

"What are you gonna do?" he asked at the door.

"I'll thumb back tomorrow."

"To Pawtucket?"

"Where else am I gonna go? Practically everybody I know lives there."

"What about Pop?"

"What about him? He's my old man, DeCenz. The old fart needs me."

He shook his head. "Boy, isn't life fucked-up? Me ending up with Bunny and you with your old man."

. . .

As was the case practically every night since I'd met her, I fell asleep thinking about Jane Weston. It was still dark when I awoke; I knew I hadn't been asleep very long.

"How much time do we have?"

I sprang upright in my bed, bumping my head on my reading light. Someone laughed. I saw her silhouette in the window.

"Jane?"

When there was no reply, I hopped out of bed and turned on a light. She was sitting on Waltham's old desk with her legs crossed. I was still groggy so instead of welcoming her I stood with my hands at my side.

"How'd you get here?"

"Walked."

"Alone?"

"Yeah."

I still didn't understand.

"Did you really think I'd leave without saying goodbye?"

"Never occurred to me."

We both smiled. The sight of a happy Jane just brought back old memories and made me feel lousy. Must've shown because she stopped smiling and walked up to me. Something was prodding me to tell her to take a hike, to be cold, mean. Sucker her for suckering me. Jane lifted her hand and I pulled her to me. I felt her breath on my face. She took off her boots, I turned off the light, and we lay on my bed, on our backs, apart. For a few minutes neither of us said anything. Jane spoke first.

"Are you still going out west?"

"No."

"Why not?"

"Because you were right," I said. "I was just looking for the easy way out."

"Sorry about all that stuff I said. Especially about S.D."

"Don't be. Most of it was true."

"No it wasn't. I was just mad at you when Rafferty told me about S.D. I guess I wanted to believe it. Then I heard how he set Irving up."

I thought things over for a while and said, "Jane, I almost killed him."

"I don't blame you."

"I mean really almost killed him. I had him up on the gutter, and I was going to push him off. At the last second I realized I was doing everything expected of me. Acting like a Rhode Island redhead and ruining my life."

"Poor Irving," she said.

"You know it had nothing to do with that."

I rolled onto my side, facing the wall.

Jane put her hand on my back. "I didn't know you then, Dunph. It's . . . it's like . . . I don't have any excuses, except I didn't know you then."

She began to cry. I turned over and put my arms around her.

"It's all right, Jane," I said. "You're right, we didn't know each other."

For the first time in my life I really understood my parents. I saw how you could love someone and still choose to leave them.

When Jane kissed my forehead, I closed my eyes and slept like a baby.

The cacophony in the dining

hall during graduation breakfast reminded me of my intersection around dinner time. I hadn't noticed when the traffic simmered down, but when I looked up I knew why. Dean Mort stood in front of my table.

"Couldn't make it, eh Mr. Dunphy?"

I raised my eyebrows.

"Your father."

Everyone at the table stared at me.

"No," I answered.

"No *what?*"

"No, he couldn't make it."

Mort sniffed. "Well, Mr. Dunphy, since your family couldn't attend the festivities on this hallowed occasion then I'm sure you won't mind going to the parking lot and directing traffic for the proud parents who *could* attend."

I shrugged.

"What does that mean?"

"I'll make my way down there after breakfast."

He shook his head and smiled. "Now."

Three hours later I was out of Cornwall Academy for good. As soon as it was announced that Jonathan Wheeler had been voted "Most Likely to Succeed," I'd walked out of the chapel, not waiting for the rest of the awards to be presented. We'd already been given our diplomas so Jane followed me out onto the chapel lawn. The bright sun made the grass look absurdly green, like the plastic fuzz in children's Easter baskets.

The banner was draped between the second floors of the two dorms nearest the chapel. "Free Sirhan Sirhan!" Funderburk was trying to figure out a way to get it down before the chapel emptied. Someone had cemented the dorms' doorways shut with Krazy Glue.

She glanced back at the chapel and then at me nervously. "Uh . . . listen, Dunph, we better move away from here before everyone piles out."

Her father was inside, and the man wanted my ass in a bad way. The school had sent him a letter outlining all of our crimes, and Mr. Weston was liable to pop me in the mouth if he got anywhere near.

"He's still mad at me?"

"Hates your guts. The guy's acting like you killed his dog."

I ran to my room, retrieved two pillow cases full of my stuff, and then Jane escorted me up the main drive leading off campus. We had to walk under the sun-draped banner that Fundy was futilely attempting to reach.

"Good riddance, Mr. Dunphy," Fundy said.

I nodded and walked past.

Jane and I continued fifteen feet or so and I turned. "Oh, by the way, Fundy, I didn't really get the hash from Sodani. I got it off Wheeler."

Fundy looked like a guy who'd won the New York lottery but had burned his ticket. As we walked away, he yelled out, "Persona non grata, Dunphy, persona non grata!"

At the end of campus we stopped and looked at each other. Mrs. Weston would be searching for Jane. Mr. Weston would be searching for me. There were many things I could've said, but I just wanted to look at her, to remember. Main thing was that the wounds had been kissed. The scars would always be there I guess, but we were alive and awake and going somewhere. We would end as friends.

"Ain't you gonna say something funny?" Jane asked.

"I'm gonna miss you."

"That supposed to be funny?"

"No, it's supposed to be sad."

We held each other.

"I'd better be going now," I said. "Your father's probably getting nervous."

"Yeah."

Jane kissed my cheek and walked back down the campus drive.

"Have a nice life," I called.

She turned. "Don't say that. You sound like we're never gonna see each other again. We're just mothballing it for a while, right?"

I nodded and caught a final glimpse of her eyes.

I walked into town and started hitching. Put my bags down in the back of an old truck that was junked on the side of the road. Dozens of black-eyed Susans stretched through the skeletal remains of the wreck, reincarnating it into a wonderful flowerpot. No cars came along, so after a while I climbed into the rusty truck and waited to go home.